Fred N. Kimmel

Big John Morgan was a fine man to work for, long as a man delivered and kept free of trouble. As the newest member of Big John Morgan's outfit, Luke Barnes was more than a little proud. But Barnes hadn't counted on treachery, neither had he counted on someone trying to blast him to hell for his trouble!

THE DENVER BUCKAROO

Fred N. Kimmel

Curley Publishing, Inc.
South Yarmouth, Ma.

Library of Congress Cataloging-in-Publication Data

Kimmel, Fred N.
  The Denver buckaroo / Fred N. Kimmel.
    p. cm.
  1. Large type books. I. Title.
  [PS3561.I422D46 1992]
  813'.54—dc20
  ISBN 0–7927–0757–5 (hardcover)   91–14439
  ISBN 0–7927–0758–3 (softcover)   CIP

© **Copyright 1960, by Fred N. Kimmel**

Published in Large Print by arrangement with Donald Mac-Campbell, Inc. in the United States, Canada, the U.K. and British Commonwealth and the rest of the world market.

Printed in Great Britain

THE DENVER BUCKAROO

CHAPTER ONE

The Spider sat his horse and watched. From the high hill above the Red River of the North, he could see clear across into Canada. The rolling hills fell away before him, a carpet of green grass, waving in the afternoon sun. His mind's eye traced the imaginary line that formed the northern boundary of the United States.

Now he watched the progress of the rider coming from the north, madly spurring his horse down a broken incline that was sprinkled with jagged outcroppings of sharp rocks and large boulders. The rider lurched the horse to the side, barely missing a cruel upthrust of granite. Then, abruptly before him, loomed another huge boulder, as tall as a wagon wheel.

Horse and rider took this new hazard with a prodigious leap and landed on a stretch of loose shale. They slid in a shower of sparks as steel-shod hoofs struggled for balance; then a shout went up as six red-coated Mounties cleared the crest behind the fugitive.

As the Mounties thundered down the breakneck grade, one horse slid to its knees, but recovered to veer past the snaggled branch of a petrified tree. Unlike the man they pursued, these riders kept both hands on the reins. There was no gunfire; each man devoted

1

all his attention to the deadly zigzag pursuit.

The fugitive dashed his horse recklessly down the remaining slope, one hand holding the reins, the other arm akimbo as though he enjoyed this suicidal scramble. Now, the dangerous declivity behind him, he crossed the invisible line that a moment before had flashed through the Spider's mind.

The group of Royal Northwest Mounted Police drew up on the Canadian side of the line. But the fugitive was taking no chances, and he pushed the exhausted horse into the Red River, and presently emerged dripping, to trot his horse toward the crest of the ascent. When he saw Spider waiting there, he abruptly drew up.

Spider Lewis was an ominous sight. His shirt sleeves were nonexistent; his arms were covered from shoulder to fingertip with bristly black hair, more of which grew up his neck in front and back. Only his nose, forehead, and two oddly shaped patches beneath each eye seemed to have escaped the advance of the hairy forest. He was dressed, as was his custom, all in black. It was not difficult for one to see how he had come by his nickname.

For a moment the fugitive studied Lewis; then, with a shout of recognition, he waved and galloped forward, to draw rein opposite the fearful-appearing horseman.

'Well, well! Luke Barnes, runnin' like hell outa Canada!' said Spider Lewis. 'Let's see, now. Last time we met was in Lincoln County, wasn't it? But you was runnin' north then.'

'And you was headin' fast for the Rio Grande,' reminded Barnes.

The hairy man threw back his head and laughed. 'Ah, that I was! Tunstall and McSween was dead, Murphy was dyin' of pneumonia, and I figured the only winner was goin' to be ol' Jawn Chisum. So, naturally, I lit out.'

'How about the Kid?' asked Luke Barnes.

'The Kid? Billy's still doin' what he likes most. When I left, he had fifteen notches on his gun.' Spider Lewis scratched among his thick chin whiskers and added, 'Probably it's closer to twenty now. Things is still plenty hot down there. Baker, Brewer, Roberts, Brady, Morris, and a pile of others has gone to hell. Remember Salazar?'

'Sure I remember Salazar. I bunked with him. Did he get away?'

'Shot all to hell!' declared Spider Lewis.

Luke Barnes winced. He looked at Lewis and shook his head. 'How come you're up here, Spider?'

'Same reason you are,' said the other, laughing. 'A change of climate's sometimes good for the health ... But, say! You might be able to catch onto a good thing that I left behind me. They're a great bunch of boys, only my face got too familiar to a certain marshal.'

3

'Sounds interestin'. What's the dope?'

'Hit for Denver,' said Lewis. 'And I can help yuh along with a little gimmick I picked up while workin' with this bunch.' He searched through his pockets and presently came forth with a piece of paper. He folded it in four and tore off the corner. Then he made two long tears along the folded edges and two shorter tears between the first ones.

Luke looked on, puzzled by the whole procedure.

Spider Lewis burst into laughter as he unfolded the paper, and Luke was startled to see a cutout of a spider before him.

'Take it tuh Room Twenty-one, Denver City Hotel, an' yuh'll meet the boss. If he likes yore style, he'll cut yuh in.'

Abruptly, then, without looking back or waving farewell, the black horseman spurred toward Canada.

Luke Barnes was six feet two inches of well-proportioned manhood, and tipped the scales at two hundred. His hair was as black as a raven's and under his heavy growth of whiskers his features were rugged, and likable.

He regarded the sheet of paper for a while. Finally he folded it and carefully placed it in his shirt. The great distance he would have to travel did not bother him. For Luke Barnes had ridden through valleys and over mountains for eight years now. At fifteen he had come up from

4

Texas with a trail herd as cook's helper, doing anything else he could.

At the end of the drive in Kansas he was big and strong, and he took to the lessons that the rough life gave. The lessons were harsh, and if you flunked you wouldn't be getting a chance to take the course again. With a horse, a gun and knife a man could make his way. That is, he could get his meals and a new outfit once in a while. After Kansas, Luke had worked up to Wyoming. That was what his life was like, always on the move, new faces, new friends and new enemies; working when he was hungry and out of money.

When he was in Montana he'd had some lessons in knife fighting. He learned fast that he did not like the feeling of the blade as it bit through flesh and ground against the bone. In Nevada he found that if you wanted to talk big, you should practice with the Colt. After he recovered from the gunshot wound he spent more money on ammunition and did far less bragging.

Over in New Mexico he picked up some Spanish and twelve good reasons why you never argued with a shotgun. Down in Old Mexico he picked up a few pointers on torture, crude and refined. Of the two methods he preferred the crude.

Wherever Luke had traveled he found he had a talent for landing in the middle of a dispute or

5

range war. He was born and built for trouble and it always found him. When he rode down the street of a town his appearance left no doubt in the citizens' minds that here was a first-class fighter. If a scrap was on, offers of a job were quickly tendered.

After you heard about 'those dirty rustlers at the head of the valley,' or 'those lousy nesters across the river,' you could not move on until you tried to help. Generally, the disputes never were resolved before the time came for you to move on. Sometimes the time came suddenly, sometimes with plenty of warning. But it always came.

Now, as Luke traveled south, he reached the point where he had previously forded the Park River. He made camp on the far side that night. Five days later he forded the Missouri near Fort Randall, where he bought beans and coffee, then four days after that, he passed over into Nebraska, having given the Bad Lands a wide berth. He crossed Nebraska at the narrow part in three days, with horse and rider plodding through the rain, heads down, but at a steady pace. He followed the South Platte for two more days and forded at Kiowa Creek. Seventeen days after he had dashed over the border, he entered the outskirts of Denver.

A restaurant was what he desired and with this in mind, he pushed the horse up and down the streets, until he dismounted at a hitch rack.

He stretched seventeen days of saddle kinks from his tired body and fussed with the horse's girth and cinch.

Finally he stepped back to look the animal over and shook his head, wondering if some expert on horseflesh would not see through the drooping fatigue, straight to the heavy bone and the mighty heart. Such a person might bring others running, for surely in yonder establishment was some other wild and reckless follower of the long trails. Only men such as that rode horses like this into the ground.

But the condition of the animal belied its fire; Luke turned to go, then almost as an afterthought he picked up the trailing reins and tied them securely to the rack.

CHAPTER TWO

As Luke entered the eating place the aroma of food delighted him. The room was long and narrow, fronting on the street. There was only one door and that was on the left. A high counter of heavy plank ran the full length of the room. The planks had been scrubbed, polished and stained with food, then scoured until the surface was dark, smooth and rich. Luke walked to the extreme right end of the room and then perched on the stool next to the wall.

A thick-girthed giant in a white apron stomped up and down behind the counter, polishing it with a clean rag.

The expression of the restaurateur was jolly enough and yet the heavily jowled face and square, underslung jaw left the impression that he could chew a big hunk right out of any man.

There was one other customer in the establishment; a withered brown man with the look and hands of one who has worked with horses. He stared straight forward after his first glance at Luke. He wanted no trouble.

The cook smiled and rubbed the counter before Luke. 'You look like a man that could do with some food,' he declared.

'Mister,' replied Luke, 'I don't know what your name is, because there ain't no sign outside, but there is a smell here. That smell is steak, and I'll take about five pounds of it—rare. With maybe, oh, ten potatoes. If you got some gravy I'll need about a loaf of bread. I like my coffee, too. After that, maybe one of those pies that I see on the shelf over there would taste good.'

The cook, his jaw sagged open like a bulldog, leaned over and peered in mock astonishment at the black-whiskered customer.

'Mister,' began the whiskers very softly but building toward a crescendo, 'seventeen days ago I was standin' in the Red River lookin' *back* at Canada. I was in a hurry then, and I'm in a hurry now. Please get the food, eh!'

For a moment they stared at one another; then the jaw slacked, for the cook had seen something there in those piercing eyes that frightened him, though he had never taken water for any man.

'Stranger, my name is Jake Kearns,' said the cook. 'Do you like your coffee black?'

The third man let his shoulders fall, for he had hunched them preparing for the crashing of bodies which he had been sure was coming.

Jake Kearns strode up and down, setting out the bulky utensils and pouring Luke a mug of steaming black coffee. From the back of the restaurant he came forth with a huge quarter of beef; this he threw on the worn chopping block and with a cleaver lobbed off a steak about three inches thick, and then threw it into a large black pan of sizzling grease. He fanned up a fire under a blackened iron pot and into it he stabbed a large wooden spoon.

'I'll have to take your potatoes from the stew,' he grinned.

Luke wrinkled his mouth and nodded, winking his eye at the smaller man. 'Where is the best stable hereabouts? I've got one mighty tired horse out there at the rack.'

'Looks beat tuh me,' murmured the small man, gazing over his shoulder through the window. 'But he might be able tuh run some, eh?'

'Enoch here runs the best stable in town,' said Jake Kearns. 'He's got a fine pasture, an' there's none knows horses like old Enoch. Been around 'em all his life.'

'Well, Enoch, you take that horse right along with you and give him some feed—maybe a nice bag of barley, eh?—and there are a few spots that could use a little liniment. You could be right, old timer, that horse might be able to run some!'

Luke smiled and tossed the man several silver dollars, telling him to pasture the horse out until he returned. Then he turned once more to the cook.

'Where,' he asked, 'is the Denver City Hotel?'

Jake Kearns was in the process of pouring himself a mug of coffee, and when the name of the hotel was mentioned he slopped some of the scalding liquid onto his hand. He cursed and fanned his hand in the air.

'The Denver City Hotel is about two blocks down Front Street from the corner of South and Front. Just keep going up this street to Front, then turn to your right. There's a big sign; yuh can't miss it.'

He took a long look at Luke. 'Only if I was you—which I'm not, o' course—I wouldn't be sleepin' in a place like that. A lot o' the boys that has gone tuh bed down there didn't get up in the mornin'—know what I mean!' He raised his eyebrows and smiled knowingly.

'You mean that they had a long sleep?' sighed Luke.

'The longest,' emphasized Jake Kearns. He scooped the giant steak from the pan and threw it on the platter. He dipped the potatoes from the stew and ringed the plate; then, smiling broadly, he placed the loaded platter on the counter.

He watched spellbound as Luke discarded the counter knife and used the razor-sharp sheath knife from his belt to carve the steak into large chunks. Each chunk was the size that Jake ordinarily put in his stew. Each chunk disappeared into the hole in the whiskers and was quickly ground up and swallowed. Half the steak was gone and four of the potatoes had disappeared.

As a potato was tossed in, more coffee went down, the knife slashed through the steak, cutting the remainder into eight large hunks. The thick slice of bread Luke folded in half and swabbed in the meat gravy. Three quarters of a slice to the bite was the way he liked his bread. And in the space of fifteen minutes the platter had become clean enough to go back on the shelf.

'Now about that pie,' said Luke.

Kearns brought an apple pie to his customer.

When Luke had made a good start on it, he said: 'Mister, in my time o' servin' folks, I

11

count myself as havin' served some real eatin' men, but yo're the he-dog of 'em all! For this meal, mister, there ain't goin' to be no charge. It's on the house.'

'Well, thank you,' said Luke, 'I'll be comin' back for more. As for this town, I might be settlin' down here for a spell if things work out. Be seein' you,' said Luke, rising to go.

He wandered from the restaurant and ambled easily up the street, following the suggested route. It was dusk, and he whistled a tune as he strode along. A small group of boys gathered at the sight of him and trailed him. He turned the corner, and the group of children, as if fore-warned, stood off and stopped. They watched him as he headed down Front Street.

*　　*　　*

Luke sauntered down the boardwalk. Most of the stores were closed. Ahead loomed the hotel sign that Jake had spoken of. The people that he passed turned and stared after him and Luke knew that his days on the trail must have made him look like a wild man. Two men, tilted back in chairs at the hotel entrance, showed more than a casual interest in their glances. Luke made good note of the knife that one of them was whittling with.

Inside the shadowed lobby a sallow-faced clerk looked up.

'I'd like a room on the street side,' Luke said.

The clerk appeared surprised. 'There's only one vacancy—room Twenty-three.'

'Room Twenty-three, eh?'

'That's right. Ah, would you like to have a bath?' asked the clerk with the slightest twitch of his nose, 'I can have some water sent up.'

'Why, yes; that would be just fine. Say, can you tell me who has room Twenty-one?' Luke asked.

The clerk looked up with a start and then turned to the key rack. With his back to Luke he said: 'Room Twenty-one is the office of a local business man.'

'I see. Well, if you'll have the water sent up, I can get some of this trail-dust off my hide.'

Luke went up the stairway but as he reached the upper landing the hair on the back of his neck began to crawl. The hallway was shadowy and even darker than the lobby downstairs.

He paused before room Twenty-one and fumbled in his shirt for Spider Lewis' paper. Bringing it out, he raised his other hand and knocked on the door. Although he could hear nothing, his senses told him that someone was inside. He was about to turn back to his room when he caught the slightest movement of the door knob.

As the door eased open a crack Luke instinctively crashed back against the opposite wall, Colt in his fist. There he stood, one hand

13

back on the wall to get his balance, with the gun poised and aimed through the crack in the door. The crack grew until at last it revealed a smiling, bowing Chinese.

'I came to see the chief,' explained Luke as he stopped and picked up the paper. He slid the gun back into the holster.

If the Chinaman had any fear of the gunman that had come to the door he did not show it. 'So solly—boss not here now. Will be here in morning. Can come back in morning?'

'Sure.' Luke turned and walked to his room.

Inside, he threw himself on the bed, until the hotel boy began to bring the hot water. When the tub was full, Luke locked the door and stripped. His gun he placed on a chair close to the tub. The long knife he placed near his feet under the water. Thus prepared, he leaned back in the tub and relaxed for an hour before which he arose and dried.

Bathed for the first time in many months, he retrieved the knife from the bath water and placed it below the bed pillow, with the point stuck into the wall. The long Colt revolver he nestled beneath the pillow also, but on the right side. This would seem like precaution enough for most, but Luke Barnes went a little further. He smashed the drinking glass and spread the sharp fragments along the window sill, then he wedged the chair beneath the doorknob. Thus prepared, he fell on the bed and was at once asleep.

Voices in the corridor and the street noises from below awoke him; he judged that he had slept until about ten o'clock. The sun was shining in through the window as he splashed water on his face and slicked back his hair. He dressed quickly, and walked to the door of the next room. There he knocked and waited.

The door opened immediately. Two men were in the room; the door-opener stood aside and waved him in. As Luke passed this first man, he took in every detail; one professional recognizing another.

Once past the first man, the figure behind the desk occupied his complete attention. Luke instinctively recognized this man as the greater danger.

Their eyes locked together as in a spell. Luke fastened his gaze on the eyebrows of the other not daring to look lower, and while he did not want to be stared down he felt he was licked from the start. He noticed, too, the great wide shoulders beneath the black coat. The man would be around six feet four tall; the waist of the giant would be small by the way that the doeskin vest tapered down. The great gold chain that looped across from pocket to pocket was the heaviest gold chain he had ever seen.

The man stood up from his chair and came toward Luke with his hand out. The body of the man was a marvel of lethal grace and

15

suggested a cougar's movement but it was the head that most impressed Luke.

The eyes—large, black and far apart—seemed each to contain a diamond sparkling in their depths. The secrets in those eyes were locked deep, and from the first brief staring match Luke knew that to try and read the man's thoughts would be the sheerest folly.

The nose was straight; the mouth at this moment engaged in the most charming of smiles, and Luke felt that many men and women had been entranced by it, as he himself was, just then.

Luke reached out to shake hands and said: 'My name is Luke Barnes. I've brought this from Spider Lewis, who said I might be able to work for you.' He passed the paper to the other.

The big man took the paper, nodding his head in recognition. 'Well, Mr. Barnes, we know something of your qualifications to work for us. It seems that there are some men now associated with me who have crossed paths with you.'

He paused and returned to his desk where he opened a box of cigars and offered one to Luke. Luke declined, and the big man deftly prepared one for himself. He struck the match and immediately the room became alive with the fragrance of prime tobacco.

'In your travels you have built up a reputation for dependability,' the man

16

continued. 'But you haven't been a success because you have been associated with petty men who held petty dreams!'

Luke nodded, realizing that this was not altogether untrue.

'Actually, Luke, I was delighted when you walked in the door just now, for by coming to us you have at last chosen the right side. Your good fortune will also be mine, and I think that your decision is one that will lead to riches beyond your wildest dreams.'

'Sounds good to me,' said Luke. 'Just about what I've been lookin' for.'

The eyes of the chief went hard as he leaned forward. 'Fine. All I ask is that you obey orders, no matter how they strike you. You'll find that the pay is good and you'll have respect wherever you go. When you ride down the street people will point you out as being associated with me. If you're in trouble they'll help you. Life is going to be easier for you. After a little training in the ways that we operate, you'll be one of us.'

'What kind of "training" do you have in mind?' asked Luke.

'Training that you'll take to like a duck takes to water. You'll be at home in the kind of work that we'll be doing. In the meantime, Ace Dawson here will fill you in on things and keep you posted.'

The boss reached into the desk drawer and

drew out a neat stack of paper money—evidently it had been precounted, for immediately he handed it over to Luke.

'Here's expense money. If you do a good job there'll be a bonus. We pay for what we get, and that way everybody's happy.'

Luke folded the bills in half and stuffed them into his pocket. He noted that the top bill was a fifty.

'Our business, Luke, has consisted of many schemes since I formed our little organization some years ago. Principally you might call it a joint venture among men of courageous spirit, aimed at exploiting certain loopholes and absences of the law that occur west of the Mississippi.'

Suddenly Luke wondered if he had just received a clue as to the identity of the big man, for the other obviously thought that Luke knew his name. The big man continued:

'Now there are those people who have said that some of my more widely known adventures would have been hanging offenses back East. However, you've been around the country enough to see my point—that it's no crime to separate someone from that which they came by illegally. It depends on what angle you view it from.'

'That's true,' Luke admitted.

'One thing you'll have to grant, Mr. Barnes. You've never heard of a dirty job being

18

attributed to Jack Morgan.'

Luke stiffened when he heard the name. He realized, of course, that he should have known when he walked into the room. Jack Morgan—adventurer, soldier of fortune, gunfighter, was a legend that had burned its name like a brand on the West of the eighteen-seventies.

What legends had spread about the operations of the great Jack Morgan! He had become known throughout the West by various flattering and descriptive nicknames. To some he was Handsome Jack; to others he was known as Honest John. Many deeds were laid at his door; some bad, some good; all were daring and imaginative. Almost as well known, of course, was Ace Dawson—the faithful watchdog that guarded the approach to Morgan.

No one had ever been anxious to face Handsome Jack in a fight. Especially after it became evident that one had to earn his way to Morgan by first cutting down Ace Dawson.

'One thing,' said Luke. 'I'll quit anytime I please. There's some things I won't do!' Luke smiled at Morgan, inwardly hoping that the leader would not read that smile for what it was—a cover-up for the clammy feeling he had inside. Also, he remembered Dawson, standing behind him.

Morgan smiled and shook his head knowingly. 'Of course,' he said, 'the door is always open. But if you ever go, be sure that you take no more than you have earned!'

Luke turned to Dawson and offered his hand. They shook, and of one thing Luke was sure: Ace Dawson had the most neatly trimmed, thin black mustache that Luke had ever seen. And the gun rig that supported the twin holsters on his hips looked smooth and fast.

'Be ready to move,' said Dawson. 'You won't get much notice.'

'I'll be ready.'

He stepped aside from the door, and Luke passed into the hall.

As he hurried down the stairs to the street, he heard Ace Dawson laugh aloud, and Morgan's low-voiced talk continuing.

CHAPTER THREE

Luke fished the wad of bills from his pocket and counted them. There were twenty fifty-dollar bills in all.

One thousand dollars! More money than he had ever had his hands on in his life. Was there ever another man like this Honest John Morgan? He headed for the nearest store. If one was to be an associate of Handsome Jack there were certain things needed.

One could not, for instance, be found in the company of the likes of Ace Dawson with the crummy old saddle that Luke possessed. He picked out a moderately priced job with some fine decorative carving and large silver conchos. He tried out one of the new model Winchesters and decided that it might come in handy for some hunting when he wasn't working. He bought two new outfits of clothes, and a beautiful pair of high-heeled boots with fancy carving.

A new saddle blanket should go with the saddle, and a fancy red-and-white braided bridle. His attention kept wandering to the small case of hand guns on one of the counters, where a new engraved Colt with carved ivory grips caught his fancy.

'Beauty, ain't she?' the storekeeper asked, taking the sleek revolver from its setting.

'The Colt Patent Firearms Company sent one to every dealer to keep on display—guess they figure all that engravin' will catch the eye. 'Course most o' the boys around here are pretty used to the forty-one an' forty-four calibers. This one here is forty-five. I suppose those fancy grips caught your eye, eh?'

Luke had his hand extended for it. 'How much?'

'Oh, it's not for sale, but the regular model here sells for fifty dollars.'

'I sure would be obliged if you'd sell me this here one.'

'Oh, no I couldn't—'

But at last he found that he could, for a hundred and fifty dollars, and Luke laid his old gun reverently on the counter, his mind flashing through the past. He was not a sentimental man, but it seemed like parting with a long-trusted friend.

He slid the long sleek Colt down into the leather holster; the fit was perfect. He quickly drew the gun and hefted it this way and that. Then he sighted across the street and snapped it several times, noting the slight deflection due to a stiff trigger pull. Suddenly he tossed the weapon spinning at the ceiling. As it came down he caught it by the butt—the first time he didn't quite get a firm grip and he had to grab for it—but the second time it thudded solidly into the heel of his palm.

Finally he seemed satisfied and returned the gun to its holster.

'Wrap the old gun up, and give me four boxes of these forty-fives,' said Luke. He poured a handful into his pocket and poked five shells into the cylinder of the gun. He arranged for the more bulky things to be delivered to Kearns' restaurant, feeling like a rich man as he peeled off the fifty-dollar bills to pay the merchant.

As Luke started down the sidewalk he marveled at the quiet of the street. The saloon

22

hitch rack held three fast-looking horses that hinted at thoroughbred breeding. And directly behind this same hitch rack Ace Dawson was tilted back in a chair.

At Luke's approach, Dawson spoke in a low voice: 'Keep yore eyes open, Barnes; you've got trouble!' This warning he delivered with scarcely any movement of the lips, his stare held straight ahead.

Luke gave no sign of recognition but the little hairs on the back of his neck began to crawl. With his right hand he eased the leather loop from the hammer on the new colt. His thoughts raced back to Dawson behind him; the idea came that he might be the trouble!

Suddenly, twenty feet in front of him, the swinging doors of the saloon burst open and a blur of a man confronted him. His two guns were already out as he cursed at Luke.

'Barnes, you dirty rat!' he snarled, and then the guns were exploding in his hands. Luke staggered back as though hit by a battering ram. He pulled the Colt and fired wildly and too late. One of the two-gun man's bullets had knocked him staggering, another had ripped through his shirt. One slug clipped a wood splinter from the wall near his face.

Then, miraculously, the two-gun man was down on the boardwalk, and Luke wheeled to face the shots that were coming from across the street. Two men were shouting as they fired and raced toward him. One came from slightly to the rear, and at an angle that almost made him look as though he were coming to Luke's aid. Luke did not hesitate in snapping a warning bullet toward the man's legs. The man went down, then Luke realized that the gunman had tripped in a rut during his wild charge across the bumpy street.

The other had stopped about twenty yards away, and now brought his gun down steadily, taking the first deliberate shot of the wild fracas. Luke sent another bullet in what seemed like a leisurely fashion after the first three shots. The deliberate aimer spun backward in a cartwheel, his gun flying from his hand. He lay still. The whole action had taken possibly fifteen seconds.

His back to the wall, packages grasped tightly in his left arm Luke quickly glanced up and down the street. Heads were beginning to pop out of doors and windows. Men drifted up to and stared at the dead. All were careful not to make any sudden movements toward the survivor and his smoking pistol.

Luke noted that Ace Dawson was now standing, his chair kicked aside, and near his feet lay the fresh cigar with smoke slowly curling upward. It was clear enough to Luke in that moment that Dawson had had no hand in this affair; that in fact, he had been guarding Luke's rear. Shifting the Colt to the hand that held his packages, Luke worked the extractor rod, ejecting the four spent cartridges and then poking new shells into the cylinder.

He holstered the gun as Dawson came to his side. The crowd parted to make way for a bustling fat man with a star on his chest.

'Well, well! So Mr. Luke Barnes, himself, has come to Denver, eh?' said the sheriff, perspiration standing out on his brow. 'Mr. Barnes, I've got to take you in for triple murder, it seems. When I got the word last night that you'd arrived, I said to myself that we'd best be havin' a talk about makin' yore stay here a short one.'

He paused to mop his brow with a large red bandanna. After one look into the eyes of Luke, he avoided further pursuit of that topic, and continued: 'Now here yuh've gone and got yoreself in a mess like this! Well, sir, we've got a strong jail here in Denver, as you'll find out.'

'Hold on there, Sheriff! I saw the whole ruckus, an' it was clear self-defense,' said a bystander.

'Yeah,' yelled another man. 'It was three agin' one—*they* jumped the stranger, here!'

The sheriff turned to the little man who had spoken first, pulled him to the center of the group and patted him on the back.

'Henry, you say that you seen what happened here. Well, speak up, man—and the rest of yuh galoots be quiet.'

'Well, Sheriff,' began Henry, 'I stood right there lookin' out of the window of the saloon. This fellow here at our feet had been standin' by the doors there, a-lookin' up and down the street. Suddenly I see that he had drawed his guns and was about to jump out the doors, and I see this big guy comin' along with these packages under his arms.' The little man paused to clear his throat and enjoy his moment of glory.

'This fellow,' he continued, 'at our feet with the bullet in his throat, he jumps through the door, guns blazing—right into the path of the big stranger, here. At that range he couldn't have missed. It even seemed like he hit the stranger here and knocked him staggering back. Of course, now I realize that the stranger was actually dodgin' them bullets.'

Luke looked at Dawson and saw the other frown at this remark.

'Anyway,' continued the eyewitness, 'the stranger here, plugged this dead hombre right in the throat—first shot! Then, turnin', he gets the man comin' across the street behind him!'

He paused for breath, his eyes shining, with the crowd straining to hear every word.

'Accordin' to Clem here,' he said, 'who flopped that guy over a minute ago, he's shot right square through the heart!' There was an appreciable murmur from the crowd. 'The third man, seein' his buddies fallin' down all around, hesitated to take aim. When he does, the stranger puts a bullet right in his ear and sends the other gent spinnin' like a wagon wheel! Those are the facts, Sheriff.'

The crowd muttered excitedly as Henry finished the story.

'Well, Mr. Barnes,' said the sheriff, turning toward Luke, 'it sounds like you go free. I'll take Henry's word any day—but I'll repeat what I said before: make yore stay here a short one!'

'Just a minute, Gus,' said Ace Dawson. 'Yo're trying tuh make out like Barnes, here, is a killer, when by rights yuh should be hoistin' him on yore shoulders an' shoutin' his praise!'

The sheriff looked astounded at this and tilted his head.

'Yuh should take him home an' introduce him to yore wife and kids,' Dawson continued. 'Folks ought to change the name o' this town to Barnes. But no matter what yuh did, Gus, yuh couldn't repay the debt yuh owe Luke Barnes for wipin' out the last o' the Sundown Gang!'

'Now, Ace, don't get riled,' purred the fat sheriff. 'I believe what Henry has told us here. As fer this bein' the last o' the Sundown Gang—that sure is good news, too!'

He looked at Luke and reached out to shake hands. 'I'm sorry that I spoke as I did, Luke, and here's my hand on it.' He turned to the others and said, 'When old Gus makes a

27

mistake, he admits it!'

Luke shook hands willingly enough and smiled at the crowd, but the sheriff was still full of talk:

'You boys give Mr. Barnes a wide berth fer a while, hear? He's goin' tuh be mighty jumpy about people sidelin' up to him fer a couple o' days. I guess every man here will agree that he's done us all a mighty good turn by wipin' out this pack o' wolves!'

A cheer came from the crowd, and the three-hundred-pound sheriff raised his hand for silence once more.

'Now, Mr. Barnes did a man's work, and the rest of us will show him some respect and do the rest of the chore. Here, you boys-toss these bodies on that wagon over there, and haul 'em to the undertaker's.'

The sheriff waved good-bye to Ace Dawson and Luke. He moved off, bossing the crowd, giving lots of advice but doing little actual lifting.

As the crowd followed after the wagon, Luke turned to Ace Dawson. 'I guess I'd 'a' been a goner for sure, if you hadn't set me up with your warnin', Ace. Thanks.' He offered his hand.

Dawson ignored the gesture. 'We stick together, Luke, so don't thank me. Mexican Joe, one of our boys, told me that the Sundown Gang was in town an' askin' about yuh. I never

28

saw the Sundown bunch so I took a seat near those three big horses and watched. Yuh did some damn fine shootin'—o' course, I see that yuh aimed at the one man's legs, an' when he stumbled yore bullet took his heart, instead.'

Luke was amazed that Dawson had caught the fast action, but he merely nodded his head.

'These people will give yuh plenty of elbow room now—and that might be good fer Morgan,' Dawson continued. 'The funny thing to me was the way that yuh moved backward from that first fellow—fastest thing I ever saw. How come the gang was lookin' fer yuh, anyway?'

To Dawson, Morgan's segundo, the important thing was not the sudden attack with its grim ending, but rather the possibility that the affair could, in some way, benefit his chief. Luke marked this before he spoke.

'About two years ago,' began Luke, 'we had a little shoot-out down in Las Cruces. Mike Terrocca, the real brains of the Sundown Gang, and his brother Steve were both killed. They'd come ridin' into town from the west with the sun at their backs, like they always did. If you ever tried to look into the sun as it sets, you can see that they picked themselves quite an advantage. I'd heard that with Mike and Steve gone, they'd run into hard luck and left New Mexico. They were all Terroccas—five brothers, and not a good one in the lot. I guess

29

they had it in for me.'

'How did you happen to get in the fight—weren't there others, too?'

'I didn't,' admitted Luke. 'You see, I came pounding into town about three or four minutes behind them. I was eager to get to town before the bank closed, as I was carrying a big deposit for the ranch where I worked. I'd come into town by a different trail and hadn't seen their dust, but before I knew what was up, I was swingin' down the street right in behind them. Then they all started shootin'. The funny thing was that the sun was goin' down at *my* back! I got off a shot and wounded Mike, and rode right on through 'em. As I rode through one of them shot Steve. I kept right on around the corner, because I knew it was useless to look back into that sun. It seemed like everybody in the town started shooting then, but they didn't hit anything except Mike who was down on the ground. Later, they counted thirty-six holes in his hide. The rest of the gang rode back into the sun, without horse or rider being hit. But they left Steve and Mike behind them, dead.'

'Just happened accidentally to ride into town after them, eh?'

'That's right.'

'An' you just fired one shot, eh?'

'So help me, it's the truth!'

'Shot their own brother, an' blamed you for it, huh?'

'Yep.'

They paused now at the entrance to the hotel. Luke looked at Dawson to see if the other was satisfied.

Ace regarded the new recruit critically, trying to break through Luke's deadpan expression. He took a fresh cigar from his pocket and bit off the end, struck a match on the door jamb and lighted it. Drawing deeply, he blew forth a cloud of blue smoke. In all this time he never blinked his eye or broke his stare. Finally, seemingly satisfied, he looked down the street.

'Tomorrow,' he said thoughtfully, 'we're taking a trip on the train, Luke. We'll take the hosses in the stock car, so yuh'll need yore trail outfit.'

'I'll be ready,' promised Luke, turning into the hotel.

As he hurried up the stairs he squeezed the bundle under his arm. Somewhere in the package was a captive 41 caliber slug that had struck the sturdy frame of the wrapped-up old revolver. He smiled, recalling that Ace Dawson could not understand how he had gone backward so swiftly outside the saloon.

At dark he checked out of the Denver City Hotel, and on the advice of Jake Kearns took a room at a boardinghouse near the edge of town...

★　　★　　★

31

Luke awoke at sunrise, washed, dressed and slipped from the boardinghouse. He went directly to Enoch's Livery Stable to look at his horse. A few days' rest and good feed had done wonders for Baldy. The horse was in a large fenced field next to the stable. There were several other horses grazing near his own.

Baldy's head pushed up and the pointed ears pricked forward as Luke approached. He trotted over at Luke's whistle, his gait silly and playful as he pranced to the fence. Heads together, the two friends talked for some time; Luke had lots of praise and a few lumps of sugar for the horse. Baldy nodded his head, trying to strike the man with his muzzle; when he did give Luke a sharp crack on the head, Baldy whickered triumphantly. This was a game they had often played in the mornings.

'Oh, you like it here, do you?' said Luke, as the horse abandoned him to run to the side of a large gray mare browsing nearby. Luke picked up a little stone, threw it playfully, and hit Baldy in the rump. The horse gave a little jump, and looked disgustedly back at his master.

Luke laughed, and walked on toward Jake Kearns' restaurant where he ordered breakfast.

After working through two platters of steak and eggs, he lighted a cigar to enjoy with his coffee. He was on his third cup before the customers had thinned out enough for Jake to take a break.

The big cook smiled as he sipped from a mug. 'Well, Luke, you've got a reputation now 'most as big as yer appetite, eh?'

'Seems that way.'

'Your things come from Wilson's Store last night after you left. Looks like a saddle an' travelin' gear?' He said this like a question.

'I'm leavin' town today, on business,' Luke said.

'I hear that you an' Ace Dawson are kinda friendly,' said Jake, winking. 'That means yo're workin' fer Jack Morgan.'

'Anythin' wrong with that?' asked Luke, smiling.

'What could be wrong with hookin' up to a man that holds a mortgage on practically this whole country?' Jake shook his head. 'Strange thing is, though, that the people Morgan has broken or forced out are few and far between. There's plenty that owe him overdue, but Honest John ain't one to foreclose.'

'I'm takin' the train today,' said Luke, changing the subject.

'Then yuh better get movin' 'cause there's only one train—the nine o'clock goin' west.' He hurried from the room and returned with the saddle and rifle, plus several bundles. These he tossed across the counter to Luke.

33

'See you when I get back,' Luke called from the doorway.

At the fence by the livery pasture he tried to persuade Baldy that the time had come to leave the big mare. Finally he snaked out the new rope. It was a bit stiff, yet he worked up a loop and dropped it over the stallion's head. Then it was but a matter of minutes until he had the stamping, frisky horse resplendent in the new trappings.

He slid the Winchester into the saddle scabbard and swung up into the new leather. At a smart trot they headed for the Denver City Hotel.

CHAPTER FOUR

At the hotel, he noted five big horses at the rack. As he got off Baldy and hitched the reins, he gave them a closer look. He was proud of his mount but those he saw at the rack were Baldy's equals.

They each stood fifteen hands and taller. They were built along the same lines, with long sloping shoulders, deep chests, powerful necks and long-boned legs that spoke of speed and stamina. Luke told himself that a lot of thoroughbred breeding had gone into the formation of these fine animals.

As he started up onto the porch, Ace

34

Dawson, followed by four men, came through the door.

'Hello, Luke,' greeted Ace. 'Moved outa here kind of sudden, didn't yuh?'

'Good mornin',' answered Luke. 'I feel better close to the edge of town, where I'm located now—force of habit I guess.' He grinned at the group of men, sizing them up in his mind's eye as a salty crew.

'Luke, I want yuh tuh meet these boys,' said Ace, putting his hand on the shoulder of the nearest man. 'This here is Mexican Joe; yo're already owin' to him, somewhat, fer spottin' thuh Sundown Gang.'

'Howdy Joe. Sure glad you were around yesterday,' Luke said. 'Gracias, amigo.' Joe was a big, handsome Mexican, and his clothes were of the fancy charro cut, from below the border. Luke had extended his hand.

'De nada, senor,' the Mexican smiled. He waved the hand aside as if, indeed, it were nothing.

'This fellow is Red Calhoun,' Ace continued. 'He's got a little temper when he's riled, but he's a good man to have at yore back.'

The redhead stuck out a big freckled paw with a wrist as thick as a log. 'Glad to have you with us, Luke,' declared Red Calhoun, then he stared down at the hand that Luke had just shaken, trying casually to work the bones back into place. His eyes held a look of respect for this new man.

'This here is Ben Bascum, he knows a thing or two about explosives. You may have heard of him as Boom-Boom Bascum.'

Luke stepped up to Bascum and shook hands. Of the five he was the least impressive, but apparently this talent made him valuable.

'The other fellow here is Pop Winters,' said Ace putting his hand on the shoulder of a towering old mountain man.

Winters was tall, straight, and built to weigh around two hundred pounds. His long white beard came to a point on his chest; his silvery white hair hung to his shoulders. He wore breeches, shirt and moccasins of softly worked buckskin. Of all the men gathered there, he struck Luke as being the standout. His bright blue eyes sparkled from his brown, leather-like skin, and when he smiled his teeth appeared to be those of a man of twenty. Pop Winters, however, ignored Luke beyond a brief glance, and went to check his horse.

At Ace's command they all mounted and started up the street, cantering abreast through the town toward the railroad. The dust tumbled and rose in little clouds behind them; heads turned and watched as they went by.

Store clerks and merchants stared with a far-away look in their eyes—it was plain that they, too, were riding there alongside those fighting men. Young girls turned and stared unabashed. The men rounded the corner and rode into the railroad freight yard; then the dust caught up to them, and for a moment they were lost in it.

When the dust cleared the horses had been lead into a waiting stock car. Ace Dawson quickly explained to Luke that the animals were to be left saddled, and that Pop Winters would ride in the stock car with them; it was the last car on the train.

The others had disappeared, going forward to the coaches. Ace gave Luke his ticket and together they walked to the nearest coach. They had just gotten seated when the whistle emitted a few staccato yelps, and the train started its slow, jerky, movement forward. Twenty minutes later, the long lonely whistle blew as they passed the last farm and lined out across the open prairie.

★　　　★　　　★

The coach rattled and swayed along the track. Luke and Ace Dawson occupied one of the last seats, and Boom-Boom Bascum was in the middle of the car with his back to them. Forward, the big sombrero of Mexican Joe told Luke that member of the group had seated himself near the front.

Ace slouched down and pulled his hat over the eyes, feigning sleep, while whispering to

37

Luke what was about to take place. The plan was to leave the train after it had covered a difficult stretch of country they were now passing through. Then they would strike out with the horses for a short distance, and intercept a very special stage that was making a run from Leadville.

Inside that stage, according to Dawson, was a fortune that belonged to Morgan and the gang—a fortune that had been discovered by a U.S. marshal—though cleverly hidden. The goods that had been 'impounded,' as Dawson put it, were not stolen, but suspicion had mounted with their discovery on Morgan's property. Of course, Morgan could claim it by identification, but this would mean answering some questions that the U.S. marshal would want to ask.

Morgan had chosen the simplest way out—he would merely take the prize back by means of a clever, well-timed strike at the stage. There would be nothing to question anyone about.

Luke dozed off, thinking of what Dawson had said, and it seemed only a moment before he was looking into the merry eyes of Red Calhoun. Beside him, Ace Dawson glanced expectantly at Calhoun.

'It's nearly time,' said Red, motioning with his head toward the horse car. 'I'm goin' outside.'

The three of them went onto the platform.

The wind roared in their ears as the train thundered through the afternoon, and overhead the black smoke from the engine trailed away with an occasional spark glowing red. There was no use trying to talk above the noise.

After a short while, the train began to slow down, then came to a stop on a sharp, jug-handled curve. Luke glanced up the left side of the train and saw that they had stopped for water and wood. The riders leaped off the train and began to slide open the big door of the stock car.

Pop Winters appeared from inside the car, and tossed the reins of one of the horses to Ace Dawson. The animals eagerly made the short jump to the ground. In seconds the four men were mounted and leading the two other horses up to the rear platform.

Bascum came through the car door, then cautiously got down and climbed on his horse. Mexican Joe stood at the door so that he could watch the occupants of the car, one hand upon the big butt of his .41.

The Mexican made a flying mount from the platform to the saddle, and the horses flew from the train, cutting in a diagonal direction from that which they had come. A minute later they dropped into a dry wash and disappeared from view of the train. Here they drew up the horses and listened. As the train began to chug away, they headed the horses up from the coulee and struck out across the prairie.

In five easy miles they pulled up in a clump of cottonwoods, where the men dismounted and adjusted their saddles. Luke noted that Pop Winters, with amazing agility, had climbed quickly to the top of one of the tallest trees, where he surveyed the country to the north. The silver-haired man descended in half of the time he had taken to climb the tall cottonwood.

'It's about a mile up the trail, with no out-riders,' Pop Winters told Dawson. 'Two men on the box, one carrying some big artillery.'

Ace frowned. 'There was supposed to be a mounted guard of at least ten men!'

Luke started at this. Morgan, who had planned the job, had sent six to take ten! That was proof of the caliber of men he was riding with; Luke decided.

'Let's take our luck as we find it,' said Boom-Boom Bascum, as if stating a proverb to himself. He crouched down and began to unwrap a small oilskin package. The other men lounged against trees or rested on the ground. Luke never saw a calmer bunch.

'Boys,' said Ace, 'when they come around the curve, we'll be all around 'em. Joe will shoot the lead horse. They'll have their hands full, trying to keep from piling up; there won't be time for any defense of what's inside.' He winked at Luke and smiled.

Luke checked his new Colt and noticed the others making similar preparations—all except Pop Winters. It then occurred to Luke that the old mountain man knew the exact condition of his weapons, and Luke also felt that there were a few unseen tools of destruction concealed among the buckskin garments. Then the noise of the approaching stage stirred the men toward the horses. As they began to mount, the Mexican vaulted onto his horse and spurred away through the trees, toward the sound of the stage.

Seconds later the coach plunged into view, the horses struggling and lunging against the collars as the vehicle rounded the curve. To the rear and coming up fast was Mexican Joe, clinging to the horse, his rifle raised. A puff of smoke from the muzzle, and the horses were engulfed in a melee of flailing hoofs, clouds of dust and the screams of animals.

As the dust cleared, Luke saw that some of the horses had regained their feet, but one was obviously dead, and another was down with his back legs broken by the wheel. The Mexican, by some miracle of skill and balance, now sat close to the backs of the'driver and guard. His Colt revolver muzzle was at the backbone of the pop-eyed guard.

'Okay, gents,' greeted Ace Dawson. 'Yuh know what we're here fer, so rest easy. Then my pard up there won't have to hurt yuh.'

41

'It ain't healthy for you to touch what we're carryin', stranger. There's a mounted guard coming along behind, and they're sure to get yuh,' declared the driver.

'Get the box out, Red,' said Dawson ignoring the driver's advice. 'Make it quick.'

Red Calhoun was in the coach, struggling with a medium-sized iron chest. This he tumbled out onto the ground. Ace Dawson tossed a noose over the box. Then he dallied the rope around the saddle horn and backed his horse, towing the box about fifty yards from the coach. Meanwhile Pop Winters was among the stage horses, getting them quiet and untangling harness.

Mexican Joe had disarmed the guards and had searched them. Then, searching the rest of the stage, he climbed down and took the reins of his horse from Luke, who had stopped the animal before it had been frightened off.

Ace Dawson motioned to Luke. Except for having shot the horse with the broken leg, he had played a small part in the activities until now. Dawson told him to ride up the road to the bend and keep his eye peeled for the approach of the mounted guard that the driver had mentioned.

Luke cantered Baldy up to the bend and stood in the stirrups, gazing up the road. Sure enough, a group of riders was spurring toward him. No doubt they had heard the shots. Luke called back to Ace that they were coming fast.

Resting in the saddle, he turned to the stagecoach. Boom-Boom Bascum was working carefully over the box, packing something in the crack around the cover. The chain that crisscrossed the box was held by a giant padlock, and to this he fastened a small white bag. Moments later he stepped away a few yards and turned his back. There was a puff of white smoke followed by a low boom, and Luke watched the cover rise slowly straight up in the air, do a little flip, and came down to one side.

From that distance it had appeared weightless, but Luke remembered differently. Boom-Boom and Dawson ran to the box and began putting the small leather bags into the saddlebags of the horses. Pop Winters had been busy through all of this, and now had a new set of wheelers in harness and a new set of leaders. The two dead animals having been cut out, the stage was ready to roll again.

Pop mounted his horse, which Luke saw had already been assigned its share of the loot, and rode to Ace Dawson. They talked in a low tone, and Pop reached down and patted Dawson on the back. Then Pop shouted to the stage driver and, firing his old hog-leg pistol into the air, he sent the coach off at a fast pace, galloping alongside and cursing the driver for more speed.

Ace looked after the old man for a moment,

then mounted and rode to Luke. He looked up the road at the group of riders who were urging their horses forward and firing some shots. They were out of range, and Ace Dawson turned and said:

'Here are three pouches yo're to get to Jack. We're all riding off in a different direction—every man for himself. Never bring a hot trail into Denver with yuh, no matter how long yuh have to stay out.'

'Who's coming up the road?' Luke asked, slipping the pouches into his saddlebags.

'While you was up here watchin', the driver said that Marshal Abe Leach is coming with ten men. They've been tailing the stage ever since it left Leadville, but Marshal Leach thought that it wouldn't be hit for the next twenty miles, so they had a late breakfast at Miller's Crossin'. He'll be plenty mad when he gets here.'

'Which way are you going?'

'I'll be headin' for 'em, only off to their right. They'll be wantin' to get right up here, full strength. Pick your own trail, Luke. See yuh in Denver.'

Luke watched as the leader of Jack Morgan's picked crew rode off.

A cry went up from the approaching riders. Shots sped toward Ace Dawson, but no riders branched off to give chase. Right for Luke they poured, a long line of shouting riders coming on

44

abreast, a huge cloud of dust billowing up in their tracks.

Slightly to the fore rode a strange-appearing man, mounted on a great brown horse. Ramrod-straight he sat the saddle, and he neither seemed to bob up and down nor sway, despite the pounding pace. The brim of his high-peaked hat was plastered straight back, and it was obvious to Luke that the man was almost a skeleton. His long, thin face and high cheekbones were accentuated by the drooping mustache and scrawny neck.

As Luke watched, the man in the lead drew his pistol and began to bring it down in a overhand sweep. Unlike the others, he had not bothered to fire when they were out of range. The puff of smoke was followed by the report of the gun. When the little piece of Luke's hat brim fluttered down past his nose, Luke knew that the time had come to move.

As he swung Baldy into a gallop, the second bullet whistled by his ear. Then he surmised that the skinny fellow with the accurate pistol fire was none other than Marshal Abe Leach, renowned tracker and U.S. peace officer. He was right.

When Luke reached the first rise, he gazed back at his pursuers. As he had expected, they were bunched about the dead horses and empty treasure box, pushing their horses here and there to pick up sign. Actually, their horses had obliterated all the traces and the rolling dust had done the rest, but through all of this Marshal Abe Leach's voice could be heard directing the effort.

On the other side, Luke saw the stage racing back toward the scene. Pop Winters, Luke thought, had gone on his way and the driver had turned back to meet the guard.

Through the edge of the dust and milling riders, Abe Leach rode. Halting his horse he looked for a long time at Luke from the rim of the hill. As the dust settled, Luke noted that the riders were formed up once again behind their leader. He watched Marshal Leach directing the men with movements of his hands and words he could not hear, then five of the riders branched off and headed up the trail in the direction that the stage had taken. The other five, led by Leach, started down toward Luke. The possemen's horses had had a good run and they were too late to overtake Luke at once, so Leach did not mean to press his quarry too hard.

The chase was on.

CHAPTER FIVE

Luke looked back from the hill, and saw he was the target that Marshal Abe Leach had selected. At first he was proud that he should be the one chosen from the group of men that had participated in the daring raid. But after the second day of trying to keep ahead of the stubborn pace that the marshal was setting, he began to feel less enthusiastic.

Luke tried every trick he knew to shake the obstinate pursuers. He attempted to cover his trail, hoping that his delaying tactic would win him at least time to rest. He soon lost hope of this, however, and on the fifth day, haggard and tired and half-starved, he dismounted behind a clump of undergrowth, hobbled Baldy, and waited with his new Winchester ready. He watched the men as they rode up the trail. They were spaced out now, and Abe Leach rode doggedly in the lead, studying the tracks as he came.

He stopped and held up his hand just before Luke's Winchester fired. The men and the marshal cursed and hollered as two of the mounts went down. The three mounted men flung themselves to the ground, sending their horses scurrying for cover.

It pleased Luke to picture Abe Leach following his trail with five men and three horses. As he took the hobble off Baldy, he patted the horse and assured him that times would soon be better.

On the sixth day Luke watched with envy as the marshal and his riders, now mounted double, stopped far below him at a lonely ranch. The posse bargained for horses and supplies; but when they were all mounted up, Luke was heartened to see the two men whose horses he had killed turn back. Leach and the three remaining men came on. At dusk Luke hung back, and toward dark, when he saw his tormenters stop and build a fire, he decided that he would pay them a visit.

In the black shadows, Luke picked his way cautiously among the great boulders surrounding the marshal's camp. Keeping down wind of the tethered horses, Luke spent nearly an hour working his way toward the camp. At last, scarcely daring to breathe, he was close enough to feel the warmth of the fire and to hear their conversation.

'Wal, no; I don't think he'd try to sneak up on us when we're like this,' said Marshal Abe Leach. 'He's tired, too, after six days and he's going to rest any way he can get it, even if it has to be out there with one eye open. He knows that we'll keep a watch all night.'

'I say that the sneakin' yellow rat would do anything, an' I can't wait to get a rope on his neck,' one of the trackers said, spitting into the fire.

Luke winced.

'He sure is slick. I thought we had him that one night,' said another.

'Yeah,' answered a man in a black shirt. 'Imagine us crawling darn near five hundred yards on our bellies, scrapin' knees and gougin' our elbows. Jus' as we gets within three hundred yards of 'im, he gets up, gets on that darn horse of his, and sprints out of sight.'

Luke frowned uneasily. He remembered moving on suddenly on several nights, but he did not know what occasion they spoke of. This, however, gave him new insight into the determination of Leach, who was apparently willing to crawl a great distance on his belly just for the pleasure of getting his man or shooting him in his sleep. Chills ran up Luke's spine.

'How's those beans comin', Bill?' asked the marshal. 'Gimme another cup of that coffee.'

Bill, the man in the black shirt, stirred the food and tended the blaze. He poured a cup of coffee for the marshal.

'Who do yuh reckon he is, Abe?' asked another man.

Luke noticed that the marshal grimaced as though he dreaded the question, but he was too honest to avoid a direct answer.

'Hard to say, Harry. When that box was discovered by those kids playin' in the abandoned Jones Mine, I didn't know what tuh do. Ya see, that property is actually owned—' He hesitated, looking at the weary faces. '—That property is owned by Jack Morgan.'

'Well—of all the damn dirty tricks!' hollered Bill, standing up. He raised his filled tin cup above his head and dashed it into the fire. Then he turned and gave the rock on which he had been sitting a kick that he would remember for days.

'Hold on there, Bill,' said the marshal. 'I ain't finished yet. I sent a telegram to my chief describing the contents of that cache. The chief decides to have a look at this stuff, 'cause it might be valuable evidence. But he realized from the first, just like I did, that Jack Morgan's so popular that nobody'd want tuh be caught even near that box, once they found out it likely belongs to him.'

'Yuh mean that's one o' *Morgan's* riders we been chasin' all this time, Abe?' asked Harry, spilling coffee as he tried to steady his shaking hand. 'And, accordin' to the stage driver, there's five *more* of 'em around here!' He glanced fearfully at the looming shapes of the rocks which cast great shadows about the firelight.

'Abe, you dirty skunk!' said Bill. 'I told yuh I'd never take the trail agin' Jack Morgan. You know about my Ma, and how he helped her!'

'I know,' said Abe quietly.

'That goes double for me, Abe,' said another. 'You know that Jack Morgan holds a past-due note of mine, and that he never charged me a nickel's interest. I've told you that many a time, damn you!'

Abe nodded. 'I know that, too,' he said.

'By God, I quit!' said Harry. He turned,

picked up his blanket and saddle, then strode angrily toward his horse.

'Me, too,' said Bill, gathering his gear and limping away.

The other man lingered on his haunches, staring at the marshal. 'I'm sorry fer yuh, Abe, but yuh shoulda told us.' He shook his head, looked sheepishly at the lawman, then hoisted his saddle and started after the others.

Abe Leach spat into the fire, as if to say Good riddance!

Luke stared in disbelief as the men saddled up, grumbling about the deceit of a certain marshal who, moments before, had held their respect and loyalty. He swallowed, seeing the Adam's apple in Leach's skinny throat working up and down as he stared into the fire. The lawman made no effort to argue or plead with the others. He looked like a very tired old man. But also a very patient and determined old man, as he reached for the coffeepot, refilled his tin cup, and lighted up a cigar.

Luke smiled in admiration. He wanted to step out and pat the old man on the back. The horsemen had already left, the sounds of their going fading into the night.

Winchester at his hip and muzzle tilted level with the brim of Marshal Abe Leach's hat, Luke stepped from behind the rocks into the firelight. He expected the other to jump up or

51

show some surprise, but the man moved not a muscle.

'C'mon in—don't bother to knock!' said the rack of bones.

'Looks like the odds are considerable more even now,' Luke said, sitting down opposite the lean old lawman.

The Marshal remained immobile; only his faded gaze moved, observing the carved boots, the new Winchester, the new Colt. Finally his eyes locked with those of Luke Barnes. For an eternity they stared, and Luke tried not to blink. Just as it seemed that tears would stream from his straining eyes, Abe Leach glanced into the fire.

The marshal answered Luke's remark by saying, 'The odds are the same—*skunk*!'

'How so?'

'Yo're a crook, an' that makes everybody agin' yuh. You all end up the same—either doin' the dead man's prance under a cottonwood limb, or bleedin' your life out in the dirt, with a dozen lead slugs in yore ugly carcass.'

Luke hefted the rifle slightly, his lips thin at this bleak forecast. The marshal caught this movement.

'Oh, I know ya think ya got the world by the tail right now—an' maybe ya have! But the world ain't havin' any part of ya, Mr. Snake. Someday soon that tail will switch and you'll be swatted to hell. When that happens, ya know what you'll do? I'll tell you: You'll come yelping to the law fer help, like a kicked yaller pup. You'll say, "Don't let 'em lynch me—keep that mob away from me, Marshal! Ya gotta gimme protection!" I see it happen time an' again. You skunks that been makin' a fool of the law are the first to cry for it when you're caught!' He paused, panting for breath.

'My name is Luke. Not "Skunk" or "Snake".'

'Yore name is *Mud*!' stated the marshal, spitting into the fire.

Luke threw his head back and laughed. 'You sure are an ornery old cuss! How about dishin' up some of that food—with no tricks on the side.'

The marshal dished up a heaping plate of food and filled a cup for the unwelcome guest. From the small folding oven he took some biscuits which he passed over to Luke, and then he fixed a small quantity of food for himself. They ate and stared at one another and from time to time the marshal looked at Luke and chuckled to himself.

'What's so funny?' asked Luke around a huge mouthful.

'You an' me bein' here like this, eatin' together, when two hours ago I was a-doggin' yer trail, trying to run ya down! Now *I'm* your prisoner!'

Having said this, he began to choke. Next he

53

broke into a roar, clutching at the bandanna at his throat in a fit of coughing and laughter. Finally the marshal sputtered down to silence, breathing heavily. Beads of sweat stood out on his brow, and Luke passed him a cup of coffee.

'Drink this, Old-Timer, it'll fix your throat.'

'Thanks—*crook*!'

'I'm no crook,' Luke growled. 'I ain't denying that I been mixed up in some shootin' scrapes, but that wasn't dishonest. It depended on the angle you looked at it from.' Luke scowled at his host, trying to make it plain that he really meant it.

'I've worked for the law too,' he shouted, 'lot's of times. An' I wasn't proud of some of the things *the law* made me do!'

'Yo're goin' to work fer the law agin, *Crook*!' said Marshal Leach calmly.

★   ★   ★

As Luke worked his way through two more heaping plates of food, he pondered these contradictory words of the skinny old marshal who sat silently across from him. He watched the expression of the man, as Luke drank four more cups of coffee and ate the last of the biscuits. Finally Luke rested the rifle on his knees and rolled and lighted a cigarette. Blowing a cloud of smoke toward the stars, he then peered at the old lawman.

54

'Now let me get this straight, Old-Timer: You keep on callin' me a crook, but now you say that I'm goin' to work for the law again. What makes you so sure?'

'I knew it when you looked me in the eye a while back. There never was a crook that I couldn't outstare, and if yo're not a crook, then you can't go on working for that thievin' rat, Jack Morgan.'

'Now look here, you can't—'

'Yes, I can,' answered Abe Leach. 'I'll call him a thief, a crook, a murderer, a blackmailer, a rat and a snake.' He gasped for breath and then went on: 'Why, I've been on his trail for the last ten years. Half of the men that I brought in during that time are workin' for Morgan. He gets 'em off with his smart lawyers and his dirty money. But as soon as one o' his men is caught, Morgan won't have anything to do with him again. Up to then, he takes good enough care of them, so the fools think that they're satisfied.'

'I don't believe it,' declared Luke.

'You better believe it, or you're dead!'

'What do you mean?' asked Luke.

'I mean that when I get through telling you about Jack Morgan, even if you don't believe me and go back to see Jack Morgan, you'll be dead in ten minutes! Morgan can look right inside your brain and know that you'll be thinking about what I said. Then, before you

55

can blink, he'll have Ace Dawson or the Mexican or Pop Winters or Red Calhoun shoot you right through the heart—from behind.'

'You know 'em all, eh?' said Luke, amazed.

'Sure I know 'em, and I know Boom-Boom Bascum who did the dynamite job on that box back there. He was an honest man once, but Morgan knows talent and the price that it takes to buy it.'

Luke sat up a little straighter, bewildered by the accuracy of the marshal's identification of the raiders.

Leach sat staring into Luke's eyes, a faint smile playing about the corners of his mouth.

'You see, son,' the marshal continued, 'Morgan hasn't been a hog. He's smart enough to spend the money that he has coming in from all around on the merchants and ranchers. That makes 'em friendly. To others he loans money on their property and charges interest. He ain't ever too eager to collect, and they love this. But look at it like this: he stole the money to begin with, so he can afford to be generous. The big thing is that he lends the money to honest people and they kill themselves trying to pay him back with interest. If folks fall behind in their payments, they quickly spread it around how Honest Jack Morgan gave them extra time to pay. Every time he does this, he makes ten friends. Those ten friends tell ten more, and first thing ya know, he's got a thousand friends.

Once in a while a feller who's mortgaged to him gets wise to Handsome Jack, and tries to tell what he knows. That's sure tough luck for him.

'The minute that one of these people opens his mouth, the grapevine tells Jack Morgan or one of his "Inner Circle", and the next thing you know the man goes broke, goes to jail, dies real sudden, or just disappears.'

'How can Morgan do all this?'

'Easy. First place, he's popular. You saw a sample of that tonight. Popular enough that people won't trade with a merchant or businessman after the grapevine says that Jack don't cotton to him. Or maybe he's a rancher, and one night his herd decides to move on. The next day he ain't got no cows and he's broke. If Morgan decides that he knows too much and has got to be shut up quick, then one o' his Inner Circle draws the short lot and the gent is efficiently taken care of.'

The marshal studied Luke's face and seemed pleased with the expression there. He spat into the fire and continued:

'The next thing that happens to this poor feller is that Honest Jack Morgan reluctantly has papers served, taking his property. Of course, all the folks know that Jack gave the feller every break, because Jack saw to it that they would know. Then the poor galoot gets the fool notion to take a pot shot at Jack or one of the collectors. Fer this, they throw him into jail. He rants and raves, but nobody believes him; he was naturally prejudiced against Honest Jack because Jack had to foreclose his mortgage. Jack's got friends in jail too; and many a man has been killed in a prison ruckus, or died behind the bars, of mysterious causes. One way or another, Jack gets 'em.'

'You said he has money pourin' in from all around?'

'I know that he has hundreds of people workin' for him. He knows what banks the money's in, he knows what stages it's moving on. He passes the information to gangs that can use it, and he gets paid back. He's in on all the big land deals, and most of them are snake-crooked. He'll even murder for money. When the job is big enough, he sends his Inner Circle and they're tough enough to handle anything or anybody.'

'But how does he get away with it?' asked Luke.

'Don't forget all the money he makes lending the swag to poor widows, and chargin' interest on it. Don't forget all the hotels and saloons and gambling places that he owns outright. Then he's mixed up in smuggling and running dope across the line. Oh, he's got the front for all this, but underneath he's rotten clear through. Someday I'll get him, or he'll get me!'

'Why is it so hard to get evidence against him?' Luke asked.

'Because, you fool,' drawled the marshal, 'you saw what happened when we impounded one of his caches. You even helped him lift it. You saw what happened tonight with the posse-men. I knew I had to tell 'em soon, because I figured that you was workin' around to sneak into Denver. A hundred times I've followed trails into Denver and a hundred times the trail has petered out. They've sneaked men past my nose in and out of that town more times than I'd care to tell you. And when it comes to smuggling, whether dope or gems or people, none can touch Lee Tong, that Chinaman friend of Morgan's.'

When the marshal tossed in the name of the smuggler, Lee Tong, Luke lost all doubt that the man spoke the truth. The Chinaman had been the one evil-looking thing that Luke had noticed associated with Jack Morgan. Now the mention of the Chinaman began to kindle a hatred in Luke, and this hate was for Jack Morgan. Still, there lingered about the man a hero's image, and Luke wanted more proof.

'So far, what you been sayin' has been mighty interestin', Marshal,' said Luke. 'If you can prove it to me, then I'll ride all the way with you. We'll get Morgan, if I have to draw my last breath doin' it!'

'Get your saddlebags then,' said Marshal Leach, biting off a chew of tobacco.

Luke stepped back through the boulders, still holding his rifle, but somehow trusting that the marshal would not try to shoot him. Soon he reappeared, carrying the saddlebags.

He sat down again, took three buckskin pouches from the saddlebags, and placed the rifle within reach. He fumbled at the drawstring on one of the pouches and looked questioningly at the lawman.

'Go ahead,' the marshal drawled. 'Open it.'

Luke removed his bandanna, spread it before him on the ground, and emptied the contents of the first pouch into it. This was a hoard of small gold coins, mostly five- and ten-dollar gold pieces. But the total was enough money to buy most men.

Luke looked over at the marshal; it was apparent that the contents of the pouch was no proof to Luke's mind. Then the contents of the second sack was emptied out onto the kerchief.

Both men gasped as the precious stream tumbled forth. Calm as Abe Leach had been until this time, he now uttered a little cry as he scrambled forward to the pile on his hands and knees. For here were rings of every shape and size. Rings of gold, silver and platinum; rings with rubies, sapphires, diamonds and pearls!

Marshal Abe Leach cursed as he sorted through the pile. He lifted each ring and squinted through the band toward the fire. Those that he had inspected, he put in a separate little pile.

Sometimes he sighed and set the ring down in a new pile; at other times he merely grunted and threw them in the other. At last the old man turned to Luke and pointed to one of the piles.

'There's yore proof right there. Listen to this.' He raised a ring and squinted at it through the fire-light. Slowly he read the inscription: '"To my darling wife, Mary, from Bill, 1865."'

The marshal stirred the rings with a bony finger and came up with another. 'How about this one: "To our daughter Sally, June, 1869."' The lawman handed over a fistful of the rings to Luke, who silently examined them.

Some of the rings were worn; others were practically new. Luke turned them this way and that, reading the little messages of love and affection. His face saddened as he handed them back. Luke could not help feeling that the rings had been taken by force from their owners and had come into the possession of Jack Morgan by devious means; otherwise why had they been hidden away in an old mine shaft? Luke raised the third pouch and fumbled with the string.

As he tipped it up, both men gasped at the yellow stream of tiny nuggets. Luke cursed as the nuggets came to rest—for the sack had contained gold teeth. He imagined how Jack Morgan had come into the possession of these pieces of the human body—artificial though they were—and chills prickled along his spine.

'I reckon I believe you now, Marshal Leach,' Luke said.

'You've got to believe me now, Luke. Because Honest Jack would kill you on sight for breaking the seals on those pouches.'

'What seals?'

'See that little bit of wax on the string there? Suppose yore curiosity had got the better of you out there on the trail, and you'd studied those knots and decided you could retie them just so. You didn't know that Morgan does his own packaging when he makes one of his little deposits like this one. If you walked in and tossed those bags on Handsome Jack's desk, he'd take one look—and you'd be dead!

'He might reach in his pocket to reward ya' and come out with that little pocket-size Colt that he hides there. Before ya could wink you'd have a lead slug for an eye.

'Or he might let you turn and start for the door. Then he'd touch the little spring clip on his forearm and that long steel Arkansaw tooth-pick would slide into his hand and whirl through the air, and he'd pin you to the door jamb right through the back!'

Luke scratched his back against the rock.

The marshal paused and smiled. Luke had

broken the seals—and in so doing, had broken down the last bridge that could lead him back to Morgan!

CHAPTER SIX

The next morning Marshal Abe Leach awoke early and, gathering wood, built up the fire from the coals. He bustled about, and Luke awoke to the smells of bacon frying, biscuits baking, and coffee boiling.

He grinned sheepishly as he yawned and stretched, marveling that he had not awakened by instinct at the presence of the other, and leaped up, ready for battle.

Suddenly he knew the answer for it. For, as ridiculous appearing as the skinny old lawman was, you could not look into those eyes without realizing that here was truly an honest, an incorruptible man. It was this subconscious thought that had apparently lulled him into sleeping like a baby.

'Mornin', Luke,' said the marshal, a smile on his wrinkled face. 'Tol' me most of yore life story, I guess, afore ya' went to sleep.' Abe pushed a cup of coffee toward the amazed Luke, and scooped up some breakfast on one of the plates.

'Why—that's right!' Luke recalled now the

way he had recounted the history of his life. He remembered that the old man had listened intently; from time to time interjecting his own comments about various outlaws whom Luke had mentioned, and about some of Luke's fracases and shoot-outs.

As Luke dug into the breakfast, the marshal observed, 'You got some appetite for a man that just picked up the enemies you did—in less than a day's time.'

'What enemies?' said Luke.

'Bascum, Calhoun, the Mexican, Dawson, Morgan and Winters—that's all,' drawled the marshal. 'An' if that's not enough, there's about a thousand others, all awaitin' to jump up and earn the praises of Handsome Jack.'

'How come you mentioned Pop Winters last?'

''Cause he's the oldest and the orneriest—an' the one that I respect the most. He's gone through a couple of Jack Morgans in his lifetime, an' he's still around. He's nasty 'nough to go through another one yet. He's close to my own age, too, so I know that he thinks about like I do. That makes me respect him a little more than I do these younger fellers.'

'Funny,' mused Luke. 'Morgan's the one that I fear.' Then he looked at the marshal, and they both laughed.

'Well, pard, let's saddle up. We've got a long day ahead and a rough trail to travel,' said the marshal.

Luke cleaned the tin utensils at the stream. After tending their horses and saddling, they rode toward Denver. An hour later they passed a ranch and talked for a spell with the owner of the spread. It was one of the ranches that the marshal and the posse had passed during the chase among the hills. As they talked, it was obvious to both Luke and Abe Leach that the rancher was greatly upset by the sudden appearance of Luke and the lawman, together, and on such amiable terms.

As they rode off, the man sat his horse and stared after them in disbelief, then he turned and galloped back toward the ranch house. There he had a hurried conversation with one of his punchers, and a few moments later that man was spurring rapidly toward Denver, making a wide circle to avoid Marshal Abe Leach and Company.

But while the rider circled far to the right before cutting back ahead of them, the keen eyes of Abe Leach picked up the little wisps of dust that climbed faintly into the clear sky.

'Should have gone around on the rocky side of us,' he drawled. 'But, like a lot o' young fellers, he just didn't have the patience! He'll get his little story to Morgan, all right.'

'Let's catch him,' said Luke, giving Baldy a kick in the ribs. Before Baldy had leaped forward more than one bound, Luke heard the marshal say, 'Can't.'

'Why not!' yelled Luke, reining the horse in.

''Cause,' continued the marshal, still riding at the maddening slow pace, 'if you learnt anythin' from what I been tellin' you, then you'd figure that the cowboy up ahead will get at least six fresh horses 'tween here and Denver—just by mentioning Jack Morgan's name. But you and I'll be lucky to get the time of day from any ranches we pass on his trail!'

They settled down to a steady ground-eating pace. The marshal was pleasant company with his wry humor and he kept Luke entertained with the story of his life. He had been 'too homely' for any girl to consider for a husband, and he became a lawman quite by accident, when the small town in which he lived, elected this skinny youngster, as a joke, to the office of town constable.

He took the work seriously, however, and in a few years a tougher town sent for him to take the place of their recently killed marshal. So it had gone, from town marshal to county sheriff, until he had finally been appointed a United States marshal. Old Abe Leach knew his way around, all right.

In all the frontier West, with all of the great peace officers who had brought the law to the untamed country, he was probably one of the greatest. Yet he could ride through almost any town without being recognized by the honest people as one of their benefactors. Not so with the law-breakers, however. Once they looked back and saw this relentless, sagging scarecrow behind them, they had cause to remember him.

He had often crossed the trail of the men of Handsome Jack Morgan, and on a few occasions had cut the sign of Morgan himself. It was easy for Leach to discern the evil behind Morgan's facade of open-handed generosity and charity, although other decent men could only see good. And it wasn't too difficult for Marshal Leach to connect some of Morgan's known lieutenants with recent crimes. As for Morgan, himself, however, that was another story. For the years he had worked on the case, the leads always ran out just when he felt he was about to spring the trap on the crafty and powerful outlaw boss.

The discovery of this cache was the first real break Abe had gotten on the case. But now that Morgan had made his move, the marshal had only the three pouches as evidence—and of these, only the one containing the rings was of much practical use. Even these would not stand up in a court of law unless the owners or heirs came forward to identify them and tell their story. But probably not even one person would want to testify—if, indeed, legal witnesses could be found.

★　　　★　　　★

Toward evening they rode down a little slope toward a group of ranch buildings, all neatly painted, the ranchyard in order. Out near the corral, a short stocky man was pumping water into a trough. The house was nestled in a small grove of cottonwoods, and some small children were running in and out among the trees, playing a game. A woman came to the door and dried her hands on her apron, then turned back inside. The man looked up, and the children scampered into the house and closed the door. The stocky man walked toward Abe and Luke as they rode into the yard.

'Howdy,' said Luke. They reined in and dismounted.

The man cleared his throat.

'Been doin' some fast ridin'?' asked the marshal as he walked to the corral. 'That gray hoss looks plumb beat. Swap someone a horse fer him, maybe?'

'An' maybe that's none o' yore business,' snarled the man.

'No call to get your dander up, mister,' said Luke. 'We're just passing through, and we'd sure appreciate to eat with you. We'll be glad to pay, and we'll move on tomorrow.'

'You'll be glad to eat with me, will yuh?' snapped the man.

'Why sure. We—'

'You'll be glad to get back on those horses and ride on, mister. And take this old scarecrow with you. You'll get no food or water or anythin' else here.' The stocky man backed behind the watering trough and leaned down. When he straightened up he held a double-barreled, 10-gauge shotgun in his fists, cocked and leveled at Luke and the marshal.

Abe Leach spoke, his voice calm and steady: 'You can put up yore gun, friend. Case you don't know, I'm a U.S. marshal and this feller with me is my deputy. Now, if you go to shoot us, then you're a-goin' to jail or to hell—so take yore choice.'

The marshal's words had some effect on the rancher, for he slowly lowered the muzzle of the scattergun, and Luke breathed a little easier.

'All right,' said the man, slightly mollified. 'You kin water yore animals, then git gone. Morgan helped me to build this place, when the banks wouldn't look at me. Guess you'd feel the same way.'

'Shore,' Abe agreed, as he and Luke led the horses to the trough and began loosening their cinches. The rancher frowned at them for a moment, then he shrugged and slouched across the yard to the woodpile. There he put down the shotgun and began to work with a double-bitted ax.

It was easy to see that this was the spot where he had worked off many a grouch, and so he labored now. Chips flew like hail, and in almost no time he had whacked up quite a pile of cord-wood.

Abe Leach had decided that they would rest the animals here as long as the man could stand it. There was good shelter here, should they be surprised by Morgan's followers.

The ranch house door opened and the woman appeared in the doorway, holding a medium-sized sack. She paused, looking toward the man.

He glared at her angrily, and went back to his chopping. With a defiant toss of her chin, she strode out into the yard, heading straight for the marshal and Luke. As she stared up at them, they could see that she had once been pretty, and was still a good-looking woman, but lines of grief were about her eyes and mouth. The two men, hats in hand, waited respectfully.

'Please forgive my husband,' she said, 'but all he can think of is this place. I can remember other things. Take this food with you, it's all I could get together, and we have plenty more. God bless you both. At least, I'm not afraid of Jack Morgan!

'He used to come here often when I was younger, and I guess I even admired him. My younger brother lived here with my husband and our family. My brother was handsome and good, but he was fascinated with Morgan. It wasn't long before they were going on rides together—then on hunting and fishing trips, and they'd bring back their game with them.

'After a while, the trips began to get longer. My brother would be gone for weeks, and finally for months. Often he would ride in with men we had never seen before, and he began to look tired and worried. Then one day they brought him back—filled with bullets and tied across the saddle. Morgan didn't have the decency to come. He sent him with one of his messengers. Now Eddie's buried here, and I hate Jack Morgan—'

She burst into a torrent of sobs, turned, and ran back to the house.

'Thank you, ma'am,' Abe Leach called after her.

'Let's ride,' said Luke, busying himself about Baldy so that the marshal would not notice the sudden mist in his eyes.

CHAPTER SEVEN

That night as they sat around the fire eating the delicious chicken that the ranch woman had fixed for them, Luke felt that things at last were going their way. Good food was in their bellies and the coffeepot bubbled fragrantly on the edge of the coals. Luke hauled out his pipe, and they smoked and talked. They both had gotten a lift from the courage of the woman. Perhaps, thought Luke, other people would be ready to help them.

'I can see,' Luke said, 'the way she felt about Morgan. I hero-worshipped him myself, before I knew what he was.'

'You ain't got real cause to hate him yet,' said the marshal around his chew of tobacco. 'Leastwise not like many of us have.'

'How do you mean?' asked Luke, drawing on his pipe.

The marshal shifted his chew over to the side of his mouth. 'A pardner that I once had,' he began, his voice very low. 'That is, I called him pardner, though he was more like a son to me. His folks were killed by Pop Winters in a feud a long time back, and while I was away I kept the boy with some friends of mine. Bob Jones was his name.

'He was just a mite of a squallin' baby when I found him, but it seemed only a few years until he had shoulders a yard wide, muscles like iron, and a smile like sunlight. I taught him to ride an' shoot an' when he told me he wanted to go on the trail with me, I was the proudest man alive. We spent three years together, the happiest years of my life. I taught him every trick I knew—with gun, rope, and knife. He learned them all fast, an' it wasn't long before *I* was learnin' from *him*.'

The marshal wiped something from his eye and poured himself more coffee. 'Well, we got on the trail of a bunch that was mixed up in dope smugglin'. And Bobby did some real good trailin' work, until we come to a fork in the road where we disagreed as to what branch they took.

'You see, *I* taught the boy to trail, and when we had our argument I called him a stubborn fool. I thought I knowed that they wouldn't take a road straight into Denver. But Bobby didn't mix reason with sign. He had that little somethin' extra in his eye that maybe one man in a thousand gets. He was the kind of tracker that could tell the color of a man's hair and his wife's first name, just by studyin' the tracks of his hoss. That's the kind of eyes Bob Jones had.

'I don't know what he saw that day, but he could tell the way these riders went. No amount of cussin' I did could change the kid's mind. Thinkin' to teach him a lesson, I took my trail and left him there, a-sittin' his horse and a-starin' after me. But he saw that his duty to himself lay along *his* trail, and he couldn't turn from it. I'll never forget the kid's eyes, Luke, as he looked at me. That was the last time I ever saw Bobby alive.

'Later, I found out that he'd been shot to death in the Denver City Hotel, in his sleep. In Room Twenty-three.'

Luke had been avoiding Abe's gaze, but suddenly he jerked his head up. 'Twenty-three! Why, that's the same room I had! Damn those yellow, sneakin' rats! I'm going to—' But Luke never got a chance to finish.

A heavy-caliber slug buzzed past his ear and drove the coffeepot into the fire, spraying ashes, hot coals and steam in their faces. Instinctively both men rolled into the darkness as other shots rang out.

★　　★　　★

Luke recovered his breath behind a huge boulder and tried to still the pounding of his heart as he waited, his colt ready. From somewhere high in the rocks above them, a voice called:

'Yuh git 'em?'

This was answered by several negatives. Luke strained to recognize a voice.

'Let's rush 'em!' someone shouted.

Abe Leach fired at the sound of this voice, and Luke followed the same tactic. The bullets ricocheted off rock, and someone cursed.

'Dammit, they got me! Help! Over here—help!'

A few more shots sprayed down from above. Luke snapped shots at the flashes, and a barrage of bullets cascaded around them.

'C'mon, let's get 'em outa thar!' a voice called from overhead.

'Hold on,' answered another voice. 'Let's *blow* 'em out! Hey, Boom-Boom, you got yore firecrackers?' Wild, crazy-sounding laughter came down to Luke and Abe.

'Okay, boys; let's cover Bascum now,' commanded a voice that sounded like Red Calhoun's. 'He can make this job a lot easier for us.'

The rifle fire picked up, and Luke shuddered. Here they were, pinned down and surrounded by a picked crew of Morgan's men, and somewhere high above, the famous explosive expert, Bascum, was making the final preparations with his favorite tool—dynamite!

All he had to do was walk down a few hundred feet where he could lob the sticks into the nest of boulders in which they were trapped.

Luke wiggled up on top of the rock, willing to take a chance against the bullets for one shot at the man with the dynamite. Abe Leach chose the lull in the firing to sneak out to the right, dragging his Winchester by the barrel.

The men in the rocks above were merely shooting at rocks and shadows where they thought the two might be hiding. Strangely enough, Luke lay in plain sight on top of a large rock and still no marksman had spotted him. Perhaps, he reasoned, it was due to some trick of the moonlight that they did not see him. Or perhaps some man had him in his sights, and was just now taking up the slack in the trigger. Luke watched until he saw the paunchy shadow of Boom-Boom Bascum working down from above.

He came down slowly, dodging from rock to rock. Finally he halted at a flat place and started to arrange his materials.

Luke tensed. Bascum had stopped just about at the edge of accurate pistol range. He cursed that he had not grabbed his rifle when the outlaws first struck, as had the marshal.

From this range he feared that he might miss Bascum in any attempt at a shot. He could neither see nor hear Abe Leach, and he prayed that the marshal had made it over the moonlit ground behind them. Or perhaps one of the shots had dropped him back there among the rocks.

Bascum appeared about set now. Luke could see him fussing with the fuses.

Bascum raised up with the first sparking missile and cocked his arm to throw. Luke steadied the shaking pistol and pulled back the hammer, then in astonishment he held his fire. For a slight shadow had flitted out from the rocks near Bascum and a clubbed rifle swung in a smooth arc. The rifle hit Bascum's throat with a sickening splat. Then the shadow dropped the rifle and moved under the first missile, which had made a little hop into the air at Bascum's interrupted throw.

The shadow made a perfect catch and lobbed the sputtering bomb upward. Again the slight figure grabbed another bomb. This followed the first, then the other was thrown. When the third was tossed, the sky lit up with the blinding flash of the first bomb.

Luke stood up and cheered at the top of his lungs as flash after flash lit up the night. Six bombs in all fell among the outlaws hidden in the rocks on the upper slope. Luke dashed over the broken terrain, climbing until he was at the spot where he last saw the old marshal, framed in the light of the bursting bombs. He could not understand how the lawman had moved into the position to belt Bascum when he did.

Luke arrived, breathless and panting, as the marshal was bending over Bascum's prostrate form. Even then the last echo was just leaving the hills, and they could hear the retreating hoof-beats of the horses.

'How is he?' asked Luke, also kneeling by the figure.

'Plenty dead,' said the marshal shortly. 'Neck's busted. Let's get up above and see what's left.'

They scrambled up as best they could. At the top they found four dead men and three horses. The rest had fled.

Wearily, they returned to the base of the hill. The night passed miserably without the comfort of fire or conversation as they huddled in the shelter of the jumbled rocks. They knew that it would be typical of Morgan's men to come sneaking back, so the two kept their hands on their loaded guns and forced themselves to stay awake.

At least they had their lives; more than that they could not ask.

★   ★   ★

At sunrise, they climbed to the highest part of the hill to survey the country around. They seemed alone for the moment, anyway, except for the dead outlaws. While they didn't feel that the attackers deserved much, they both admitted that they'd feel better if something was done. So they dragged the bodies into a rock fault in the stony section of the hill and filled in the impromptu grave with small stones and rubble.

When they returned to the base of the hill, they had coffee and biscuits and then Abe got the gear together. Luke saddled the two horses, which had somehow come through the night unscathed, although they had been hobbled nearby.

Silently they jogged along the Denver trail, too tired after the battle and the sleepless night to do much talking. One thing was eating on Luke: he was determined, somehow, to get to Morgan, and do whatever he could to stop his lawless reign. And preferably he wanted to do it alone.

There were several reasons for this, and not

because he had any desire to make himself out a hero. To begin with, he figured he owed a solid debt to Marshal Abe Leach, and this would be a mighty good way to help even the score. Too, Abe's story about the kid that was killed in the same room he himself had stayed in at the hotel, had made a growing impression on Luke. Finally, he was afraid that Abe, being a career United States marshal, would consider himself bound by certain legal and approved methods—unless he was attacked. And despite Abe's assertion that Luke was a deputy marshal, Luke knew that he was not a duly constituted official, so he would have, he believed, more latitude in his actions.

But just how he was going to accomplish the capture of the towering outlaw chief, Luke simply had no idea. Vainly he tried to cudgel his brains as they rode through the dust and warmth of midmorning. It was no use; he was too exhausted. He looked at the marshal, who was nodding in the saddle, and felt his own eyelids start to droop.

Thus, drowsily yet inwardly alert to any untoward movement behind them, they jogged along the Denver trail.

CHAPTER EIGHT

Five hours later they entered the outskirts of Denver. Abe had reasoned that here, in the very domain of Jack Morgan, would be the safest place to conceal themselves while figuring out their own tactics and strategy to be used against the master outlaw. Here, also, they would have the best chance of finding out just what Morgan's plans of action were, and take whatever countermeasures they could to circumvent them.

As the marshal talked, Luke shook his head or grunted whatever answers were called for, for his own brain was busy formulating his private scheme of attack. It was indeed a daring plan, an idea so risky as to seem foolhardy, but for that very reason—and because of its simplicity—it was just the type of attack that might work. Luke admitted to himself that the marshal might reasonably object to it. At least one thing was sure: Abe would certainly want to be included, and—even if he generally approved the idea—he would want to boss the operation, as he had every right to do.

So Luke kept his own council.

Leach wanted to purchase a new coffeepot, and he knew that a letter from his chief waited for him at the post office. This would be just the time, Luke reasoned, to put his scheme into action.

They dismounted at the post office hitch rail and stretched their legs. 'I'll get the things in the store over there and pick up my mail. Meet you back here in about half an hour,' Abe said.

Luke nodded, trying to keep his heart from pounding. 'I'll just look around for a while,' he answered.

When the marshal had disappeared into the store, Luke strode diagonally across the street, straight to the Denver City Hotel. He intended simply to walk boldly through the hotel, shooting anyone who tried to stop him. Once in Morgan's office, Luke would quickly arrest him, or kill him. But if he could hustle Morgan through the hotel with a gun in his spine, he had merely to take the man to Abe Leach. Being a federal officer, Abe could take over the town jail.

The lobby, save for the startled clerk, was suspiciously empty. His hand on his gun, Luke dashed up the stairs two at a time. Safely he rounded the corner, and reached for the knob of Room 21.

Only then did it occur to him that the outlaw leader might very well not be in the room. He could be even behind Luke at that very moment! With this thought, he almost fell into the room and gasped when behind the massive desk sat the commanding figure of Handsome

Jack Morgan. Luke had not forgotten for a minute the feeling that came over him whenever he entered the presence of the other—the feeling, strangely enough, of admiration and, to a lesser extent, of loyalty. What jury would ever convict the handsome thief? What judge would ever sentence him? Was he indeed, really a crook?

Now he felt like a bird trapped in the frozen glare of a snake's eyes—hypnotized and doomed to destruction. The outlaw was tranquilizing him with the pleasant smile, and actually disarming him! Luke hardly remembered that he was covering the chief outlaw with his revolver. But Morgan appeared totally unconscious that Luke held a gun on him. His charm and friendliness seemed to warm the room. He pushed back the paper on which he had been working, not at all surprised at the intrusion. As for the long Colt revolver aimed a half inch to the right of his heart, Luke Barnes might as well have been pointing a harmless finger at him!

'Well, well! Luke Barnes! How are you, man?' He gave his voice all the cordiality reserved for an unexpected old friend.

'Fine—no thanks to you an' your gunmen!'

Morgan slowly raised one empty hand and laid it palm down on the desk, then he placed the second hand on top of the first. He appeared too calm, and it made a shudder go through Luke.

'Stand up!' commanded Luke.

Morgan smiled. 'But I'm comfortable here, man. Take a seat yourself!' He gestured to a chair.

'Don't move like that again!' shouted Luke.

'Of course. What's up? Why the gun? Is this a stick-up, eh?' The outlaw arched his eyebrows, a look of puzzled amusement on his face.

'You're under arrest!'

'Oh? Let's see the warrant, then.'

'There isn't a warrant, but there soon will be—a federal warrant, too!'

'Oh, yes. Federal ... Ah, that troublesome old crackpot, Leach—that's his name, isn't it? Wants to question me, does he? And what right has he got to question me? I hear that he found a cache in one of my old mines. Does that prove anything, I ask you? Does that prove I stole the stuff? I'll tell the world it doesn't!'

He smiled at Luke and gave a little shrug, showing that the whole matter was nothing to him. 'Why, my lawyers would get him laughed right out of court, the skinny old fool! After this one, they'll really take his badge.' He chuckled. 'Found a cache of valuable trinkets in my old mine, did they? Well, it's my good fortune wouldn't you say?'

'How?'

'Found on my property, wasn't it? If the old

fool hadn't tried to transport it and got robbed, I'd have it!' He smiled knowingly at Luke.

'You robbed him yourself,' said Luke, growing calmer.

'Can he prove it? The bandits wore bandannas up to their eyes, I believe. Also,' he added slowly and with humor in his eyes, 'also it seems that the two drivers of the stage have unfortunately passed on. One was backed over by the coach while examining the rear wheel. As for the other chap, he cheated at poker over in Rielly's Saloon the other night. And Ace *hates* cheaters.'

When he said this he looked hard into Luke's eyes. It was clear enough that Luke's change of sides, was, to the outlaw, even worse than cheating.

'You forgot one thing—that I'm an eyewitness to that holdup!'

'By George, you're right! I have you to deal with, at that!'

He stood up, cold hatred clear on his face for the first time. He turned away, thrust his hands into his pockets, stared through the window, down into the street.

'Turn around slow, Morgan, and don't try anything,' demanded Luke.

The other spoke without turning. 'Barnes, your honest face disgusts me! All right, boys, take him!'

Luke started to wheel, but the unmistakable

feeling of not one but two revolvers prodded the flesh of his back.

Turning his head slightly he could see first the sneering Ace Dawson on one side, and then the impersonal stare of the Mexican. Dawson carefully reached around and took his Colt. But strangely enough he merely took it off cock, and dropped it loosely in Luke's holster. The way was clear for him to commit suicide by reaching for the gun, if he desired. Slowly Luke raised his hands, knowing that only the convulsive twitch of a finger muscle stood between him and death.

'Ah, that's better,' said the chief as he turned back, placing a small, nickel-plated revolver on the desk.

'Every wolf has a fang or two!' he said as he reached into a drawer. Then his hand emerged, holding two thick packets of bills. He ran the other hand through his hair and fixed his eyes on Luke.

'Barnes,' he said, 'I'm giving you this money, and you can walk out of here right now—a free man. Just go out there and shoot Abe Leach. Ace and the Mex will be close by, and you'll get safely away—they'll see to it!'

'Just shoot him down, eh?' said Luke, his voice tremulous.

'Yes. Front *or* back, I don't care! How you make the pudding don't interest me. You can go somewhere else, get a new start in the East or in Europe. We'll never bother you again. And here's the grease that'll turn the wheel.' Morgan thumbed through the stacks of bills and waved them under Luke's nose.

To Luke it looked as if there was at least ten thousand in that pile of money, although his meager experience with that substance would never qualify him as an expert on estimating its worth by the pile.

'Keep your lousy blood money!' he yelled in the outlaw's face. 'Keep the damn money that you stole from women and kids!'

Two gun muzzles dug deeper into his back, and a flush of anger spread over Morgan's handsome features.

'*You* fool! You damned, stubborn, *stupid* fool!' he exploded. 'There's thirty thousand in those stacks!'

'I wouldn't take a hundred thousand from you, you slimy, crawling snake!'

Morgan's smile was frosty. 'So you thought you could barge in here and take *me* did you? I'll show you—I'll hang you! Today!'

He threw the money down on the desk and strode to the window. 'Take him over to the sheriff and lock him up. Get a lynch mob ready at sundown!'

Luke wondered if the prophecy of Abe Leach was going to come true. A dread feeling of hopelessness came over him.

'Make sure that the sheriff keeps the posters

on him and the marshal on display,' Morgan added as they turned to go.

They started down the stairs, Dawson in the rear with his pistol snug against Luke's backbone at the waist, and Mexican Joe in the lead with his pistol jabbed into Luke's belly. Dawson steered Luke along by holding his left arm and the Mexican led him along with a grip on his right.

They reached the bottom landing, and the lobby that had been empty only moments before was now packed with twenty armed men. At the hitch rack twenty horses were saddled and ready.

They had left the long porch and were starting across the dusty street as the shots rang out.

Luke was jerked to a halt as they all gazed toward the sound of the gunfire. From the door of the post office a small thin man darted, smoking pistol in his hand. He vaulted the rail and somehow got the two horses that were tethered there in motion at once.

A second man, visibly shaken, appeared in the post office doorway. 'Help! Get the murderer!' he screamed.

Men were pouring from doorways along the street. In a split second they were leaping for their horses. Shouting, their guns out, the men poured through the door of the hotel. But those gun-hands stood paralyzed as the desperado, riding one horse and leading the other, bore down upon the unlucky trio in the middle of the street.

The plunging, flailing hoofs were upon them before Luke realized that the daring athlete that had vaulted the post office hitch rail was Abe Leach, himself.

With an agonizing scream, Mexican Joe went down beneath the churning legs of Baldy. Dawson was knocked spinning into the dust as he attempted to dodge the marshal's horse, the gun in Ace's hand exploding harmlessly in the air.

Luke found himself between the two horses where a moment before there had been no space at all. He grabbed at Baldy's flying mane and pulled himself up as they flew down the street. He was free again!

Such was the speed of the pick-up that Marshal Leach and Luke had hardly gained control of the horses when once more they found themselves fighting to stay in the saddle. At the corner of the street, their horses reared high, forelegs pawing desperately for balance, as a huge freight wagon, hauled by ten span of mules, blocked the intersections. Swiftly Luke and Abe kicked the horses around and surveyed the street behind them.

Luke, his hat gone and his shirt ripped, dropped his hand and felt the butt of his revolver, still in the holster in spite of the acrobatics. He brandished the weapon in his hand as they spurred the horses up the street, straight at the milling group of horsemen!

The town was half mobilized in pursuit; the street was a stage and Morgan had carefully placed his actors upon it. The confusion of men mounting frightened horses all but obstructed the view. Now a similar freight wagon pulled across the opposite end of the street, the driver setting the brake and jumping down to watch the fun.

Sealed into that space with Luke and the marshal were forty horsemen, half of them already mounted and waiting, while the others, on foot, tried to quiet their skittish mounts that were excitedly rearing and plunging.

The fantastic horsemanship of old Abe Leach had given them the saddle, but the advantage had been only momentary.

Now, with a wild shout, the horde of horsemen swept up the street, guns in one hand, reins in the other, to wipe out the two fugitives. But the posse, overexcited by the prospect of a sure kill, started to shoot wildly—and every shot missed.

The two madly charging fugitives, however, were more careful in their fire, and managed to down the mounts of the two foremost possemen. Fully half the armed riders sharply reined up their horses to avoid running down the leaders set so abruptly afoot, amid shouting and cursing and the stomping of iron shod hoofs. Then two more of their number fell from the saddle, clutching at their wounds.

Straight at the heart of the large, milling group bore the marshal and Luke, guns blazing in their hands. Morgan's men were at a standstill; the thought of guns at this close range was something they had not considered when they had mounted their glorious charge of a moment before.

Most of them, in fact, stayed their guns—for to shoot now was to risk killing your best friend, so tightly packed were they. The charge had been reduced to a wild bucking-horse contest, a mad melee of dust, cursing men and screaming horses.

The men that had not yet mounted that day now ran for their lives, many of those that tried to fight their plunging, kicking horses lived on as cripples. Men who had proved calm in the clutch before, now fought to hold their horses and added to the confusion by foolishly firing into the air.

Suddenly out of this swirling maelstrom burst the horse of the marshal, followed closely by Luke on Baldy. The marshal galloped his horse straight through the doors of Rielly's Saloon, ducking as he crossed the threshold. Two bounds behind him came Luke Barnes and Baldy.

'Jump!' shouted the marshal as he leaped

from the horse and slapped him out the rear door.

'What—?' started Luke, then followed Abe Leach's lead.

'Over here,' yelled Leach as he threw himself down behind the bar and squeezed beneath a shelf of glasses. Luke pushed himself under the shelf with difficulty.

Outside someone was shouting: 'In Rielly's Saloon! They went into Rielly's Saloon!'

'Some of you men on horses get around in back—they'd go right through!' shouted Ace Dawson.

Several men rushed into the room and raced through, pointing to the dents left on the smooth floor by the shod horses.

'Right out the back door they went!' groaned one of the men.

'Just a cloud o' dust up the street—that's all that's left o' them two!' said another man, coming back in the rear door. 'Got clean away up the street thar—no tellin' which way they turned off!'

'What's this?' snarled Ace Dawson, running into the saloon.

'Jumped those hosses right out the back door an' into nowhere!' exclaimed one of the crowd.

'Yo're *all* nuts!' roared Ace Dawson. '*Nobody* could ride a hoss out of that door!'

'But *they* did it!' said another voice. 'Rielly was out there, and saw the whole thing!'

Luke stared perplexedly at the marshal, who winked back.

'Did Rielly tell you that to yore face?' queried Dawson.

'Sure did!' said the other.

Dawson cleared his throat. 'Well, Joe, if Rielly said it—then I reckon it must be so!'

Luke puzzled over that remark, and at the same time he wondered who the Rielly was, for Ace Dawson to accept his word without checking, and on the word of another, at that.

Apparently Rielly was never known to have lied. But it was equally apparent that Rielly just had! Why did Rielly lie, Luke asked himself. This Rielly must surely be a man of great integrity to so impress these scoundrels. He wanted to meet Rielly someday—if he lived!

'Here comes Jack Morgan on his big white horse,' yelled one of the men at the door. There was a rush of feet as those in the room crowded to the doorway fronting on the street.

'Hi, Jack!' yelled a bystander.

'Howdy, John,' called still another, eager for recognition from the personage. Ordinarily Jack Morgan would have gone a block out of his way to return the salutation of either of these unimportant men. He knew that the surest way to make a friend was to call him by name. But now popularity was of second importance to him, for he was sure that by personally leading the pursuit he could turn failure into success.

92

Therefore he called out in an authoritative voice:

'You men on foot! Search all the surrounding buildings. Look behind every curtain—under every bed. A thousand dollars for the first man that sees them!'

A cheer burst from the crowd as they rushed eagerly to the search.

'Yes, sir!' yelled one of the men. 'We'll turn 'em up!'

'Good! Ben Wilson, I knew I could depend on you!' said the leader from his prancing white horse, and he gave the man a look that every other man present envied.

He added: 'The rest of you men mount up—I've organized twelve groups of eight riders each! Comb the streets for them! They're both wanted for the murder of the whole Howard family at their ranch, two nights ago! A thousand dollars to the first mounted man that sees them!' he shouted.

Now Luke could get the meaning of what Morgan had said when he had made his remark about the sheriff and some posters. The posters, of course, were for him and the marshal—branding them both as family killers! Another rotten, fantastic scheme perpetrated by the master crook.

The Howard family would be the family of the woman who had given them the food. The vengeful Morgan had murdered them, and framed Luke and the marshal for it! Luke felt helpless and he blamed himself for the death of the innocent people.

'We'll turn this town inside out! We'll find them before the night is over!' promised Morgan. 'And when we do, we'll have some quick rope justice!'

Having thus charged the group before the saloon, Morgan swung the big charger about and doffed his huge white hat to the crowd. Then he leaped the horse down the street, giving orders to this group and that along the way. Another group of mounted men dashed up to him and hollered something, pointing off in another direction. A shout went up and they all pounded up the street, led by Morgan.

'Well, their goose is cooked, now that Morgan himself is bossing the chase,' observed one of the men still in the barroom.

'Let's get started with the search, boys,' said Ace Dawson, ruefully rubbing his cuts and bruises. He glanced across the bar into the mirror, muttering and grunting, and leaning closer to survey his battered features.

Luke and the marshal stared up at the close reflection in the mirror, and it was if they were staring directly at the man himself. If he ever looks down! thought Luke and he snaked his revolver out from under him.

Ace Dawson turned to the other man standing at the bar. 'Well, Bart, aren't yuh goin' tuh do some lookin'? Or are yuh that rich that a thousand dollars ain't worth tryin' fer?'

'Haw, haw! You know, with my lousy luck, Ace, I couldn't see 'em if I was standin' on 'em!'

Luke gulped as he heard Dawson's feet shuffling around to the end of the bar. Was he coming to collect the reward himself? Had he seen them in the mirror, after all?

The dusty boots walked to within a foot of Luke's face. Then they turned and walked back again to the other side of the bar. Luke heard the clink of glass against bottle, and a moment later Dawson's face again appeared in the mirror. He poured himself a whiskey and gulped down the fiery stuff straight.

With Dawson sitting on one of the stools now, the saloon became so quiet that the hidden men could hear each other breathe. It was only a matter of time until the gunman looked into the mirror, or until he heard one of them breathe—then he would start shooting, and it would all be over.

CHAPTER NINE

Dawson yelled suddenly, jumping back from the bar as someone moved a piece of furniture near the door. 'Oh—it's you, Rielly.' He returned to the bar and poured himself another whiskey.

Rielly made no reply but continued to move the chairs and tables back into their proper places. From the way that the furniture was spinning about the floor, Luke assumed that Rielly was peeved about their riding horses through his saloon.

'You know, Rielly,' Dawson said, looking around, 'I'd a-swore that no man could've rode in here and then rode out the back door as fast as those two did, accordin' to the boys. And I'd a-swore that the boys was lyin', but when *you* backed them up—well, then I had to believe it!'

Rielly closed the back door but said nothing.

Luke winced at the thought of the great Rielly coming behind the bar, as he detected the quick, catlike step of the famed saloonkeeper.

'Tell me about it, Rielly, will yuh?' said Dawson. 'Did they really ride 'em right through the door back there?'

Luke braced himself for the saloonman's outcry of discovery as he heard Rielly coming closer. Surely the man would survey his own back bar, and see the intruders.

Rielly came behind the bar and spoke to Dawson. 'Why no Ace, that wasn't the way it happened, at all. They whipped those horses out of here, and then hid under the bar!' Rielly said with a touch of sarcasm.

Ace Dawson guffawed, slapping the wood and making the glasses jump.

Luke gasped, opened his eyes, and stared at the feet of Rielly. His ears had not belied the fact! The boots were small and dainty. And Rielly wore no pants but a skirt! Rielly was a girl—and a girl with a pretty leg, at that! But what was more important, she knew that Abe and Luke were there. She even prodded Luke with her boot when he'd made that little gasping noise.

'Haw-haw-haw!' bellowed Ace Dawson. 'That's a good one, Rielly! Why, I was back there a minute ago myself—an' I've been in this room since they rode through! Ha-ha-ha!'

Rielly nodded. She picked up the whiskey bottle and held it to the light, checking the level. 'I can see you've been here some time!'

Dawson reached in his pocket. 'Keep the change!' he said, tossing coins on the bar. 'I'll check on things.' His voice floated back as he shouted to the men across the street.

Rielly polished the surface of the bar and said in a low voice: 'Quick—you two! Out of there, and keep your heads down!'

Abe and Luke scrambled from their cramped position below the shelf and waited on their hands and knees.

'We're out,' the marshal said.

Rielly didn't look down but busied herself polishing glasses. 'Quick! Get down to the other end of the bar—move that big barrel.' Her instructions came from lips that scarcely moved as she went about her work, and waved to a passerby on the sidewalk.

'Now get—the trap door loose and get down there,' she commanded, with her back to them.

Luke watched the marshal digging in the sawdust with his knife. He found the crack and using the blade as a pry, he raised a small section of the floor, three of the boards coming up as one. The air, drifting up from the hole, was dank and musty, but to the two fugitives it was the sweet smell of freedom.

They waved to the girl, who played her part by ignoring them and fussing with her hair in the mirror. Then they dropped through the hole and closed the trap door behind them.

Rielly went to a box and began to sprinkle fresh sawdust on the floor behind the bar. When passing over the door she stamped it tightly in place. She looked at the barrel, and realizing it was too heavy, did not try to move it.

Some of the searchers, giving up, were returning to the barroom. From the sound of their voices Luke realized they were in a bad temper.

'Where's Dawson, anyway?' someone said.

'Yeah, he was goin' tuh stand the drinks!'

'Here he comes now,' said Rielly. 'What'll it be, fellas?'

'Come on, Ace, belly up—as long as you're buying!' laughed one of the men.

'Slipped away right under our noses,' muttered Dawson. 'I just can't understand it!'

'Jack'll run them down,' consoled one of the barflys.

The conversation turned to an excited buzz as the beer and whiskey warmed the bellies and loosened the tongues of the men.

'I saw the skinny old guy leap the rail at the post office and untie a horse with each hand. Then he jumped clean into the saddle—right from the ground without touchin' a stirrup!'

'Here's to Mexican Joe,' saluted a member of the group. 'May his bones rest in piece!'

'I'll drink to that,' laughed another man. 'His bones was so busted up, they got to rest in—ha-ha!'

Down under the floor of the bar Abe Leach had groped about until he found a candle and lighted it. The room was eight feet wide and twelve long and high enough for Luke to stand in. The walls were stout plank, fitted to keep out the earth behind them. The floor was rough planking also. There were two cots and a crude table between them. From the far end of the room a draft from a small door sucked steadily at the candle flame.

Placing the candle on the table, each sat on a cot and listened to the voices from the barroom. One of the voices said:

'Here come the rest of the boys, with Jack Morgan!'

They could hear the clatter of horses and the voices of the large group in the street. Some of them dismounted and came into Rielly's place.

'Well, we got their horses!' shouted the first man, coming in the door. 'Found 'em both, grazing in an empty lot about a mile from here.'

'Here's a drink to that good news, boys,' said one of the men, tossing some money on the bar.

'Here comes Jack!'

A chorus of greetings rang out as Morgan entered. The men realized that the free drinks would flow faster now, at least while the boss was present.

Even in the room below the bar Luke and Abe could sense the presence of the outlaw, and guessed that his mood was of the foulest.

'They can't get far without horses!'

'That's right, friend,' said the smooth voice of Handsome Jack, '*but* they didn't ride those horses far. At least a dozen people saw those horses running without riders—people not far from *here* either!'

He shot a quick glance at Rielly, behind the bar.

'Rielly, here, says they whipped those horses out the back door—and hid under the bar!' laughed Dawson. The others joined him in chuckling.

Rielly smiled as she went about her work.

But Morgan strode toward the rear of the bar, and everyone's laughter trailed off as the footsteps of the big man thumped down behind the bar. He examined the space carefully.

Rielly stood with her hands on her hips, giving him an indignant and puzzled look.

Morgan walked to the end near the barrel, then turned apologetically to her. 'I'm sorry,' he said, with his great head tipped to the side as though he had just sensed or heard something. 'I'm truly sorry, but you know that remark of yours would make sense—if there were any place to hide here!'

He glanced about the room again and over to the large stairway that led to the quarters upstairs. He turned to Dawson.

'Have all the buildings around here been searched?'

'Of course, Jack,' answered the lieutenant. 'All but Rielly's place, here—I mean, Rielly saw 'em go out the back herself!'

'Get up those stairs with some men and look around!'

Dawson scrambled for the stairs, followed by a dozen men.

Below the floor the two trapped men heard the crowd going upstairs. Curiously enough, the sounds came to them the clearest from the little door at the end of their room.

Above them there was a trace of scorn in Rielly's voice. 'Well, handsome, as long as you're back here, you can move that hogshead over, please. The teamsters put it right in my way!'

'Sure, Rielly,' came the Morgan's agreeable voice.

Luke watched some sawdust trickle down as Morgan applied his muscle to the huge barrel that had taken both him and the marshal to slide out of the way. The sounds of the men coming down the stairs in twos and threes drifted through the little door at the end of the room again.

Morgan spoke: 'Those crazy fools slipped through us somehow, men! I'm upping the reward to *five* thousand in gold to the man that leads to their capture! What's more, the money will be held by Rielly, here.'

This remark brought an excited murmur from the crowd.

Morgan added, 'Rielly will be the sole judge of any man's claim. Nobody could be a fairer judge than Rielly!'

'That's sure true,' shouted one of the men.

'The money will be right here in Rielly's safe!' continued Morgan.

Morgan turned to the girl and said: 'I'll stop by later. Please forgive me. I've had a bad day but I'll make it up to you!'

He replaced his hat, which he had removed for this speech, and walked quickly from the room, followed by Ace Dawson.

Luke was eager to question the marshal about the events of the day. He pressed the other man to tell him what had happened in the post office, but mainly he wanted to know about the beautiful and mysterious Rielly, for Abe Leach had never mentioned her in any of their talks.

Marshal Leach told him how the clerk in the post office had tried to plug him by suddenly pulling a concealed gun. The clerk had shouted 'Murderer!' at him when taking the shot, but the lawman did not wait for an explanation. For some reason, he had unhitched the reins of the two horses before he went into the post office; since both horses were used to being ground-hitched anyhow, he had no fear of leaving them.

The clerk had fired one wild shot, and the marshal had simply thrown a shot close to the man's ear to frighten him a little. He explained that he had no intention of taking Luke's horse, but in his excitement to get mounted he had grabbed his reins and one of Baldy's, as well. And Abe insisted that he never saw Luke and his two captors crossing the street until he was right on top of them.

Luke was inclined to doubt this, believing that the marshal was trying to be too modest about the daring rescue. But Abe protested that he would never have intentionally tried such a fool stunt, for fear of harming his friend.

Luke explained to the marshal about his foolhardy plan that he had attempted, and how he had been in the hands of the outlaws all the while. But what, Luke wanted to know, about Rielly?

She was the daughter of a former saloonkeeper, Abe told him. The older Rielly had had connections on both sides of the law; information always went to the highest bidder, and he had no scruples about selling the information twice. Then Jack Morgan had come to town and the money that Morgan paid for information—or a good turn—was too rich for Rielly to compete with.

He became a confirmed Morgan man and prospered in his business. There soon came a time when he had no debts or mortgages. His daughter was one of the prettiest girls in the town and there wasn't a boy who hadn't heard about her. Morgan had taken a shine to the girl when she was twelve, and over the last ten years her fame as a beauty had spread far and wide. Morgan, however, had always been there at the right time to discourage suitors. Naturally, the older Rielly never had a bad word to say about Morgan, so that Jane Rielly had grown up in an atmosphere of hero-worship for the handsome 'businessman.' At first, it had seemed to her, he was much too old for her, but as the years went by she came to feel that perhaps some day this dashing hero might be hers.

In the last few years Morgan had pressed for a quick marriage, but she had steadfastly refused to be rushed into it. It was said that Morgan was in the foulest of moods in the days following one of these rejections. And so Janie, as Abe called her, was living in a vacuum as far as other male suitors were concerned.

Those who were simple-minded enough to make a play for her generally left town, for some mysterious reason. Others were never heard from again. It took only a few incidents like this to convince everyone that to court Jane Rielly was a rather risky business.

Her father had passed away two years ago, an old rogue who died in bed of natural causes. His deathbed raving had led her to the discovery of the underground room and passages. He had apparently used it for smuggling years before and for a hiding place at those times when he had led others to believe that he was out of town. Then, living comfortably below his own bar, he could eavesdrop on the conversations of his customers. The information that he gathered from the tongues loosened by liquor he sold to whom it would be the most valuable.

The door at the end of the room, the marshal explained, led to a passage coming up in a small private courtyard at the rear of the saloon, and opened beneath a large, cleverly constructed flagstone. There was one other branch of the passage to the rear, and this led to her father's old room—now hers—on the second floor of the building.

Jane Rielly had come to Leadville over a year ago and slipped a note to Marshal Abe Leach right under the nose of Morgan's spies. The note had given the marshal instructions how to get to the secret passage, and in this manner he had come to know the girl personally, although he had heard of her beauty long before. She had, Abe said, confided certain suspicions about Morgan that had been growing over a period of time.

It seemed with his first proposal there arose a shadow of doubt in her mind, and she had not consented. She had at first believed that this would pass; however, with each succeeding proposal, the doubt had grown. Anyway, there was that expression in his eyes—just the merest glint—of frustrated evil.

Abe had made a half-dozen contacts with the girl since then, and she had been successful in getting the information about the cache at Leadville to him. Abe had been in this room before, but he had always come at night and by the back way.

Through all of this Luke listened attentively, and when the marshal had finished, he whistled softly. His hopes soared, now that he realized how Rielly felt about Morgan.

'Listen,' said Luke standing up, 'it sounds like Morgan's voice again!'

They stood up to hear better. It was near closing time, and Morgan had returned as he had promised. His smooth soothing voice fairly purred through the floor into their ears.

'—and we just can't go on like this, Jane dear. You've got to admit that I've given you plenty of time—time to play at being a businesswoman, time to travel, even time to get used to me!'

He went on: 'You know I've been waiting *years* for you to say that you'll be mine. We could go anywhere; New York, London, Paris! You'd be rich. We could live as and where we pleased; perhaps Italy in the winters and some cool, northern country in the summers.' Then the voice of Rielly came: 'Now John, you're just upset over today!' she said, 'so you come running in here and propose!'

'I'm *not* upset! *Damn* them!'

'But you are. And are you sure you're right? Why, I hear that this new man—what's his name? Oh, Barnes—I hear he's a fine-looking young fellow—hardly the type to shoot a woman! And Marshal Leach has a wonderful reputation for all these years! You're *sure* you've got the right men for the crime?'

'Of course, I'm sure!' said Morgan in a slightly higher-pitched voice. 'Red Calhoun is a witness, and we're keeping him in hiding until

107

we need to give proof!'

'Oh, I wondered where Red had been keeping himself,' said Rielly, her voice trailing off.

Morgan said: 'As far as this Barnes is concerned—he's got a big ugly mug and soul to go with it! After all, he took pay from me one day and then slipped off to join one of his crook friends the next—taking my property with him! Fortunately, we got that back when we found the horses this evening. He even had the audacity to snoop into some personal parcels that I had sealed.'

'You're sure they're guilty, then?'

'You'll see when we get them in jail,' he sneered.

Luke and the marshal heard him restlessly walk to the door. 'My patience is wearing thin, my dear. The events of today have me upset, I'll admit; but I think you would do well to take my advice and resolve yourself as to our future together. Because, very frankly, I'll never let another man have you!' With this remark he angrily stalked from the room.

'Good night, John,' Jane called after him coolly, and busied herself with closing the saloon.

CHAPTER TEN

A half-hour had passed when Luke and the marshal heard muffled sounds coming from the passage at the end of the subterranean room. A moment later the latch on the small door lifted and Jane Rielly appeared with a tray heaped high.

Luke sat respectfully quiet as she set the tray between them. He watched the pretty profile as she poured coffee and removed the cover from the feast. She's perfect, thought Luke, as he stared at her shoulder-length red hair, the red-gold of a desert sunset. Her skin was soft and white and utterly delightful in appearance, her limbs were well-molded. She wasn't a small girl.

The tray contained not only the coffee but a big platter of cold beef and sliced cheese. An enormous loaf of freshly baked bread and a bowl of apples filled out the meal.

Marshal Abe Leach broke the silence by saying, with an amused glint in his eye: 'I don't believe you two have met formally. Mr. Barnes—Miss Rielly.'

He paused while the two gazed at each other, their eyes holding one to the other's in admiration.

He added: 'I suppose you can see that he's a

big galoot who likes tuh get into trouble. But he can do some other things fairly well, as you've heard.'

The girl stood very close to Luke, looking down at him. Her nearness made him embarrassed to return the stare. She placed her hands on her hips and, giving her skirts a little twirl, she flounced down the room a few steps. Then she turned and once more looked him full in the face.

'Well, he might be handsome if he'd get rid of those whiskers! My, what greasy black whiskers you have, Mr. Barnes!'

'Oh, I'm not much to look at, ma'am, I mean Miss Rielly, ma'am,' Luke stammered, kicking at the floor with the big spur on his boot.

'Well, *I* think yo're plumb beautiful, Luke!' guffawed the marshal around a big mouthful of roast beef.

'Well not exactly beautiful, but nice and strong-looking,' said the girl matter-of-factly.

At this remark the color began to creep up in Luke's face and spread clear to his forehead. He tried to think of something to say, but words wouldn't come. He turned his attention to the food and began one of the famous devouring sessions that generally took place after a long separation from regular eating.

Jane Rielly, her hands still on her hips, threw back her head and laughed as the first sandwich found its way into Luke's mouth. She stared, still amused, as he swallowed an oversize mug of steaming coffee. She looked on in absolute disbelief as he bit a large apple in half and then sawed two more slices of bread from the loaf and piled in a pound of meat. From this colossal sandwich he tore a large hunk and sluiced it down with a long swig of the coffee.

'My friend Luke has got a powerful problem in his appetite,' said the marshal, looking hungrily at the empty platter before him.

'I'll get more,' said the girl, starting for the dish.

'No,' said the marshal, staying the girl with a wave of his hand. 'I'm quite full; we've got to get out tonight, if Luke is satisfied!'

'That was a fine feed,' said Luke, ignoring the sarcasm of the marshal, and addressing his comment directly to Rielly.

'Thank you,' she said. 'You must have been terribly hungry.'

He nodded. 'Why, I could stay on here a spell, if you're so inclined, Abe. The food's good, and where else could we be so close to what we want?'

'Are you sure that what you want is the same thing that you came here fer?' said the old marshal, raising one shaggy eyebrow.

'What *did* you come here for?' asked Jane, her head to one side and the trace of a smile on her lips as she regarded Luke. 'It seems that if you had trouble in mind, you've got enough of

111

it. I've never seen Jack as angry as he was tonight. Of course, when he's around me he tries to hide it, but it comes through, anyway.'

Jane then told them how talk had spread as one after another of the Inner Circle had returned to Denver and she had been able to piece together a good idea of the importance of the holdup. Prior to the arrival of Luke and the marshal she had heard of the alleged murder of the Howard family—a rumor cleverly started by one of Morgan's men right at Rielly's bar. The posting of a price on the heads of the two had quickly followed, and the town alerted to be on the watch for them.

'Our best bet is to get out of here before Morgan gets thinking about how easy we gave him the slip this afternoon. I swear that if he tries to sleep tonight the answer will come to him, and he'll tear back here and rip this place apart, board by board, until he finds us!' declared the marshal.

'What about horses?' Luke asked.

'I'll get them,' said the girl. 'It'll take some time, but if you'll wait in the courtyard, I think I'll be able to get them.'

'We can't be fussy, Jane, but try and get somethin' thet can run fast and long,' said the marshal. 'I got a feelin' that we may be a bit rushed when we leave this town of Jack's!'

'I'll do my best,' the girl said. And she left them alone in the room.

112

Luke stared after her, and in his heart he somehow knew that she would do just that—her very best. He also knew that with her doing her best for him, he would be able to do more than his best for her. He shuddered to think what would happen if he failed and she continued to be the virtual prisoner of Jack Morgan.

After checking their guns, they hesitated and then went down the passage, heading for the courtyard. The stone gave way, and Luke saw the stars above him as the cool night air tumbled into the dank passage. They climbed out of the hole and replaced the stone. Then, half-crouched, they softly ran the few steps to the high wall surrounding the patio.

Their hearts fell as they heard two men talking on the other side of the wall. A guard had been posted in the rear of Rielly's, after all. That meant that the crafty, outlaw boss had not altogether discarded the idea that they were still in Rielly's place. Some suspicion had led him to keep a guard of two men here at the rear wall. No doubt the front of the place was being watched, as well.

One of the men was saying, 'If ya ask me, Morgan is nuts to think that those two guys would still be in there—or that they'd come back here tonight!'

'I didn't ask you, Mike,' said the other man. 'An' if anybody's nuts, it's you!'

'What's here that they'd come back fer?'

asked the first man. 'I can't see how they could possibly be in the place. You was here when we searched it, Frankie.'

The approach of a rider up the alley startled the two guards.

'What's this?' said Mike. 'Who comes?'

'Ace Dawson,' came the answer from the horseman.

'Any news, Ace?' asked the guard called Frankie. 'Anything new about those two rats? How do yuh think they ever got away, huh?'

'They didn't get away,' said the chief lieutenant. 'They're right around here. Morgan's fit to be tied, but he's on the right track now. He's sent for old Bob Griswold and his pack o' hounds. They're bringing them into town now by wagon from Deadtree.'

'Did ya hear that, Mike?' said the guard, Frankie. 'They got old Bob Griswold an' that pack of wolves a-comin'. By jings, now we'll get some action! Maybe we can catch those guys, and still get some sleep tonight!'

'That's smart, alright,' said Mike. 'There'll be plenty of things on those two hombres' saddles to give the dogs the scent. Them dogs can pick up a real cold trail.'

'I sure wouldn't want that big white devil on *my* trail! What's the name of that big snarlin', slobberin' hound, the one that's the leader of the pack, Ace?' asked Frankie.

'Diablo's his name, but I never heard him

answer to any name or to anyone, for that matter. That brute and old Bob Griswold just maintain a working agreement between 'em,' Dawson said. 'Funny thing about that dog; I've seen that pack of Griswold's work a dozen times, and I never once see that dog come tuh Griswold for affection. The dog does his job, in return he gets a place to sleep and his chunk of raw meat. And that's it.

'He don't sleep in the pen with the other dogs; Griswold keeps him apart. It's not that he's afraid of the dogs—God, no!' continued Ace Dawson his voice breaking a little. 'Why, I've seen him turn on the whole pack, and silence the lot of them with three or four snarls.'

'You mean tuh say that one dog cowed that pack of Griswold's?' asked Mike. 'I've seen that pack of dogs run a few times, too. Griswold's got bear dogs, bloodhounds, and dogs part wolf, and lion hounds. There's one thing that all of 'em has in common: guts. I say that no single dog could bluff that pack—without having his bowels ripped out, pronto!'

'You say wrong, friend,' cautioned the steady voice of Ace Dawson obviously perturbed that Mike had questioned his word. 'Me, I've seen that big white devil do just that. I'd rather tackle a grizzly bare-handed than mess with that brute!'

Luke looked into the face of the marshal and he saw the concern about the coming dog pack

115

outlined there, just as it must be in his own face. Apparently they were still trapped, and the dogs would make matters worse. What should they do? He thought of jumping through the gate and attempting to take Dawson, but there were the two guards, and a commotion would rouse the town. Yet, if they returned to the passage, the dogs would surely find it, and point to Rielly as the fugitives' accomplice.

Rather than expose the girl to Morgan's wrath, he would wait until the dogs came and then make a dash down the street. The wild pack would get him in a trice, but at least Jane Rielly would be safe; for once the dogs cornered him and Abe, the animals would be satisfied.

While the marshal dared not speak with the guards scarcely a foot away on the other side of the wall, Luke could tell by the expression on Abe's wrinkled face that he would do the same thing when the dogs came.

CHAPTER ELEVEN

From the front of the building they heard the noise of an approaching wagon. It came to a halt with the screeching of brakes and the snorting of horses. The noises that came back from the front of the building also were spiked with the howling and whining of the pack of hounds.

They were here!

'Looks like old Bob Griswold and company have arrived in front,' said Dawson. 'You boys stay on guard; I'll let you know if I need you.' Dawson galloped off.

'Frankie,' said Mike, 'I've got to get a look at that big white dog!'

'Yeah? If he sees you first, watch out.'

'No, I mean it. I'll just sneak down to the corner, and look around from a distance. You keep your eye on things.'

'Set still. Ace said to guard, and we'll guard. If he tells us to look, we'll look ... Say, here comes Morgan now!'

'Heck, that ain't Morgan. It's Morgan's horse, Blazer, though. Who's ridin' him?'

'Why, it's Rielly coming on Blazer and leadin' her own horse.'

The guard walked out to take the bridles when Rielly dismounted.

'Howdly, Miss Rielly, ma'am. We're sorry we got to be here—Mr. Morgan's orders, ma'am!'

'It's all right, Frankie,' said Jane Rielly. 'I'll leave the horses for a minute. I have to go inside.'

'We'll keep our eye on 'em, ma'am.'

As Rielly pushed through the gate and walked to the rear door she gave only the slightest glance to the side. Luke and the marshal waved silently to the shadowy form.

117

But their hopes were born anew, thanks to the girl; for only a yard away stood two magnificent mounts.

Between them and the horses stood two men, but considering the element of surprise the odds were on their side and they knew it. Quickly they stepped to the gate. There must have been the faintest noise—perhaps a spur jingled—at any rate, it was lost in the confusion of the next few seconds.

'What the—' yelled one of the guards as he realized that someone was behind them. 'Who—'

He never finished the sentence. As the man jerked his rifle up, Marshal Leach's gun barked, and a spurt of orange flame licked at the guard's heart.

'Help!' the second guard shouted, the suddenness of the attack scaring all reason from him. In that moment he cracked up completely, firing his pistol wildly. Another explosion followed from Luke's gun and the man crumpled, the shocked look still on his face.

The horses reared, but Luke and the marshal had them in hand at once. Leaping in the saddle, they kicked the horses up the street at a furious pace. Luke's big white at first seemed to resist, giving several long leaping bucks, but when he dug in the spurs and gave him a hard slap across the rump, the horse straightened out and ran like the wind. Down the alley they raced and when they came to the end, they turned and rode down another dark street. A few more turns and they were passing the last few shacks on the outskirts and heading out into the prairie.

The night was clear, and high above the moon shone, round and silver, giving them almost the light of day. It was perfect for the long burst of speed they needed to get the jump on the dogs and the pursuit that was surely being organized at this moment. If they could get a long lead, they could give the horses an easier pace—that was their hope.

Luke yelled for the marshal to turn and look. There, coming out of the shadows of the town far behind, surged a large group of riders. Fifty horsemen galloped swiftly there. No; there would be around sixty! There was one sure thing—they were all well mounted and coming at a fantastic rate for such a large cavalcade.

Well up in the front rode a solitary, resolute horseman; his mount glided along, its feet seeming scarcely to touch the ground, so perfect its gallop. On the prairie that night this horse was probably second only to Blazer that Luke rode at this time. The swift, effortless action of the leader's horse gave a ghostly appearance to the pursuers.

Like the steady roll of distant thunder the sound of hoofbeats rolled across the prairie to the pair of riders ahead, echoing in their ears like approaching doom. Far to either side of Morgan's riders ranged two packs of dogs running a zigzag course as most hunting dogs will, using their noses instead of their eyes to run down a quarry. Far ahead of them, its head up and never wavering, ran a big white dog. Periodically he would let out a long wild howl.

Luke leaned forward over the flying mane of his horse and patted him on the neck. Luke could feel the great ribs spring outward between his knees; those ribs housed the tremendous heart and lungs which gave the horse the great endurance he was now showing.

The horse that the marshal rode was a hand higher than Blazer, but he conformed more to the lines of a great hunter or jumper. Luke noted, as he looked to the side, that the horse easily maintained the pace set by Blazer. He had the long sloping shoulders and the great chest that most riders would call 'heart.' Here truly were two fine horses, and the pursuing riders seemed to sense this as they deployed for a long, hard chase. With a yell, a group of about twenty men burst from the main body at a horse-killing pace, determined to get the quarry.

As Luke looked back he saw them throw away their packs; even canteens and rifles were being jettisoned in an effort to get all possible speed from the horses. They closed the gap to two hundred and fifty yards, but ten more horses were broken down—never to be worth their salt again!

Bullets were coming close, and one shot nicked Blazer. For one heart-sickening moment he lost his stride, and a shout of triumph came from the pursuers. Then the cry died in their throats as the horse quickly regained the faultless pace. Luke felt the animal for blood but found nothing. He hated Morgan more than ever; how could the man take a chance on hitting the wonderful horse?

Looking back, they could see that they had reduced the odds to about twenty to one. But the forty riders behind them still came on and had even gained in the race. The hopelessness of the fugitives' situation was apparent; before them lay miles of open country—behind them, the forty riders, and behind the forty were strung out twenty more. Then Luke stared back in disbelief as the large party came to a dusty halt.

Luke and the marshal continued on for a hundred yards and immediately slowed the horses to a walk. They could see that a hurried conference was being held by the pursuers. The group then did a strange thing. They fanned out into a long line with the distance between each rider gradually increasing. Minutes later Luke looked back, amazed to see the ground that the pursuit had lost, but the new formation struck fear in his heart. The riders were spaced apart at two hundred yards intervals and came on in a long, wavering semicircle. Luke, looking back, realized that the horns of that rough crescent extended for more than a mile. Their pursuers had formed a human net, and that net was now closing in!

★ ★ ★

'What are they up to?' Luke yelled to the marshal, galloping beside him.

'It's Devil's Canyon,' he answered, letting go with a long stream of tobacco juice at the enemy coming behind.

'Can it be jumped?'

'Can't even be bridged!' came the reply. 'They're afraid we'll try an end-run, I guess.'

'Why not try it?'

'Lead off!' bellowed the marshal.

They pushed the horses to the right and spurred wildly along a course roughly parallel to the line of the horsemen. The wisdom of Morgan's plan was immediately apparent. The riders at the end of the line, seeing the latest maneuver of the fugitives, quickly dismounted. These men flopped down in a prone position and began some uncomfortably accurate rifle fire. The first shot took Luke's hat from his head. The second bullet passed close beneath the marshal's nose, the breeze fanning his mustache. Glad to be alive, they resumed their old course, with rifle slugs still coming close. They whipped the horses forward toward the rim of the canyon.

About six hundred yards from them Luke spotted the wide, jagged streak of blackness that marked the chasm. He yelled to the marshal, pointing ahead. The marshal nodded grimly, knowing that soon they must pull up their horses and make their stand. Already they could hear the roar of the river far below as it fought its way through the tortuous, twisting channel of the gorge.

Luke raised himself in the stirrups, trying to get some idea of the gorge they were approaching. Now he could see that the sides were split far back from the edge by cracks and faults, which appeared as long, black fingers wriggling back from the rim. The depth of these splits was not apparent, but far to the left he could see that one of these defiles was running ever closer to intersecting their path at the moment.

Luke looked quickly behind. With a shout to the marshal, he steered Blazer away from the crack, forcing Sonny and the marshal to the side. Then Luke made a dash at the black void. He could only guess at how the horse would perform. To jump a horse across an opening like this was dangerous enough in the daylight, but at night it was sheer suicide. As he approached the abyss, he gave the horse its head and leaned forward over the neck of the animal.

Blazer soared from the ground and landed on the other side in a shower of sparks as the shod hoofs glanced along the rock surface. The marshal yelled a curse, but pushed the big thoroughbred Sonny after the white horse and completed his leap across the rift in the rocks.

Luke estimated that the split in the rock formation had cut off most of their pursuers. And the marshal suddenly realized the importance of his leap. The long rift in the edge of the canyon ran back for almost a half-mile. The riders, following in the semicircle, headed for the place where the split entered the canyon. But here the slit ran back at a slight angle so that its end had probably cut off only three or four riders of the big group. The rest of the pursuers were on the other side.

The far rim of the gorge had been cast higher than that on the near side of the river. At this moment the moon cast a deep shadow from the far cliff and in this darkness they walked the horses easily in the welcome concealment. Behind them they heard the cursing and yelling of Morgan's riders as the horses lunged and milled about, while the riders realized that their quarry had temporarily escaped.

The gap that they had jumped was not too wide for many of the horsemen gathered there, but desperation was necessary to attempt it, and with the odds at a mere twenty to one, not a man there felt the need to take the risk. And so, while Morgan raced his horse about taking stock of the situation, the bulk of the riders rested their horses and had a smoke. There were some words of admiration for the horsemanship of the two fugitives—but these were carefully out of earshot of the chief.

It was Morgan's idea to wait for the dogs. The trail over hard rock would be difficult to follow, and besides it was known that there were some riders on the other side of the split—but their number had not as yet been determined. The precise location of these men was also a mystery, for the plan had been to head straight for the lip of the gorge and the main party had been pushed together by the split only in the last half-mile. If these men did not spot the fugitives and raise a cry, then the dogs, surely, would soon find the trail.

Meanwhile, the marshal and Luke had dismounted and were cautiously leading their horses through the shadowy rocks near the edge of the canyon. They felt their way along, hoping not to make a noise or stumble with one of the horses. Then suddenly, they stopped and held their hands over the horses' muzzles as they heard conversation ahead. A light showed as one of the men drew deeply on a cigarette, briefly revealing three men, holding their horses by the bridles.

'Say, Tex—gimme a light here, will ya?'

'Shore,' drawled the man called Tex, striking a match.

Luke glimpsed that they were three salty-looking fighters. To try to back up would surely bring forth a noise, and a noise would as certainly hasten a hail of bullets in their direction.

'What beats me,' said the third man, 'is what happened to everybody all of a sudden—did you see what happened, Earl?'

'Danged if I know,' declared Earl. 'One minute I'm within sight of Johnny Wing, an' the next second he ain't there no more!'

'Couldn't just disappear,' said Tex. 'They musta stopped, or somethin'—maybe *they* got 'em!'

'Jack said we couldn't miss gettin' them at the river—but I don't hear shootin',' said the third man.

'Maybe they gave up,' said Earl hopefully, and then added, 'Or maybe they ran to the right and everybody chased 'em that way.'

'What's that?' suddenly asked one of the men, holding up his hand for silence. 'Sounded like a horse's hoof on rock!'

'I thought I heard a hoss whicker a while back,' declared Tex.

'There! Hear that? There it is again, Earl!' said the excited member of the group. 'You heard it—didn't yuh hear it, Tex?'

Luke's heart began to triphammer as the painful silence he was trying to maintain was shattered by the marshal's gruff voice at his side:

'Put out those damn cigarettes, Earl! Yuh want to get yoreself killed?'

The three men jumped visibly at this sudden command from the blackness in the tough, authoritative voice. Instantly three glowing butts dropped to the ground and were tramped on.

'Who's that?' demanded Tex. 'Doggone these cussed shadows; I can't see yuh, friend.'

'Dammit, Tex, keep yore croaky voice down!' said the marshal. 'Yuh want Morgan to come over and pull yore tongue out?'

Tex grumbled something about Morgan, and was still.

'Is that you, Tom Bolin?' whispered Earl, in a large voice.

'Quiet, you damn fool! I'm not gonna tell yuh agin!—I'll come over there and knock yore thick head in!'

The marshal pressed softly forward, beckoning Luke as he did so. Slowly they began to lead their horses past the trio of gunmen, edging along the scant fifteen feet that separated the three from the lip of the gorge.

As their dim shadows glided by, the cowboy named Earl spoke once more: 'Tom, can yuh tell us what happened? Did they get 'em?'

'They got the big ugly one,' said the lawman in his forced whisper. 'They're gonna wait fer the dogs to run down the old coot!'

'Where yuh goin', Tom?'

'We're taking a message tuh Red Calhoun,' lied the marshal. 'Morgan says for you boys to watch this end till the dogs come.'

'Yeah? Why should we watch this end at all?'

'Help might come.'

'Who'd help *them?*'

'Anybody—yuh damn fool, don't yuh know they're innocent?'

Luke and Abe were far enough past to mount the horses now, and they carefully walked them for a distance before swinging into a fast gallop.

The three men left guarding Morgan's right flank passed the time talking about poor Tom Bolin, and how he had never been the same since he had fallen from a hay wagon some years back. Then they settled down in the dark to await further orders from their Chief.

CHAPTER TWELVE

They put a solid three-quarters of a mile between them and the canyon before they brought the horses to a walk. They were, of course, in full moonlight once more.

'So they got the ugly one, did they!' laughed

128

Luke, slapping the marshal hard enough to break his shoulder. 'You're a foxy old coot!'

The lawman chuckled, using the time to work nervously at his tobacco plug.

A solitary yelp caused them to look back. There, running alone in the moonlight was the mighty white dog.

Luke cursed. 'Well I'll be damned! It's the big, white murderin' hound that the guards were talkin' about back at Rielly's!'

He pulled up Blazer and threw the reins to the marshal. Jumping to the ground, he squatted in a kneeling position, steadying the large Colt pistol with both hands. The dog came bounding on, teeth bared in a snarl, ears plastered back against his head and the hair bristling along his back.

Fifty feet away, thirty, then twenty, he came bounding straight at Luke. Luke's finger tightened around the trigger, another second and he expected to hear the crash and feel the gun buck. In the second that he hesitated, the dog skidded to a stop. Then, strangely, the animal lay prone and with head erect, stared across the twenty feet toward the black whiskers of his opponent. Man and animal poised with eyes locked, neither daring to waver his glance.

For two minutes they sat thus, Luke suddenly not wanting to kill the wild thing. Then the low snarl that had been coming from the dog stopped. The plastered-down ears flopped foolishly forward and the dog turned his head at a slight angle. There was something about his whole attitude that had suddenly changed. Luke barely breathed as he released the tension on the trigger. He sighed as he realized that the trigger was free and the animal temporarily safe.

The enormous dog now wriggled forward, belly dragging in the dust, a low whine escaping his throat. He edged nearer, and stopped a scant leap from Luke's throat. He growled and whined, his tail started to wiggle. It was just the tip at first, but finally the whole tail began to switch and this ultimately extended to the whole rear half of the animal. Hesitantly, then, the dog rose upon his feet. Looking right into Luke's face, he gave the black whiskers an affectionate bump with his muzzle!

'Well, I'll be damned!' declared the marshal. 'He thinks yo're his brother!'

Luke smiled silently, and gently raised his hand to pet the dog. 'Nice boy, old Diablo—nice feller,' Luke said, patting the dog on the back.

The marshal grimaced. 'Careful, now! That brute ain't no dog, he's a devil. Watch out!'

'Devil is his name, but hc's a good boy—aren't you, boy?'

The dog was now straddled over Luke's legs, muzzling and whining as if he had found a long-lost friend. Luke stood up and the dog stood up, too. They stood there for a moment, the man six-feet plus tall, the dog standing with his huge fore paws on the man's shoulders, and looking almost anxiously into his face! The devil-dog's tongue was hanging out as he stood panting steadily, and he looked over at the marshal as if expecting some comment.

'Well come on. One of yuh get on that hoss and let's get out o' here,' said the marshal dryly. Then he fished in his vest for the plug of tobacco.

Luke took the big front paws of the dog and gently placed them on the ground, then he jumped back into the saddle. The dog gave a little yip, startling the horses for a second, then he fell in step beside Blazer. They loped along at a steady pace.

'Where are we headin', Abe?' asked Luke.

'I think I'll have a look around at the Howard ranch,' said the lawman, his mouth set in a tight line.

Luke nodded, and glanced at the other out of the corner of his eye. With what he was about to suggest, he expected an uproar.

'Abe—you'll think I'm nuts, but I'm goin' back to Rielly! I'll help her get away—she'll need help after tonight.'

The marshal showed no emotion. 'Yo're a darn fool! But if I was yore age, and Rielly

131

looked at me the way she did at you—I'd do the same!'

The old man drew up his horse and they paused there on the prairie. He looked across at Luke and put his hand over on the shoulder of his younger friend. Luke was touched. The time they had been friends could be measured in only a few days, but there was enough in their memories to last a lifetime.

'Be careful, Luke. I'll meet you tomorrow night, near where we got Boom-Boom and the others. If yo're not there by ten, I'll ride in the Denver trail, lookin' fer you.'

Luke nodded. 'Good luck, Abe, pardner. Take care of yourself.'

They separated, the dog staying at Luke's side. He galloped on, then, turning in the saddle, perceived that the marshal sat watching him. Luke vowed to himself that he would return to his friend as soon as possible, and that somehow he would help him to bring Jack Morgan to justice.

He did not consider the fact that they were both fugitives from the law, legal quarry for any men to seek out and shoot in the back. Instead, he thought of Rielly, and of the fine horse beneath him, and of the dog running at his side. These new-found allies perhaps would help to turn the tables on Morgan. Exhaustion began to creep up on him and he started to cast about looking for a place to rest—before he fell from the saddle.

The terrain at the moment did not seem to offer any suitable cover so he jogged on. Slowly his eyes began to close. He fought to keep awake, but every now and then it was pleasant to nod and let the horse pick the trail. Soon he was doing more riding with his tired eyes closed than with them open. The huge dog trotted at his side and kept looking up at the exhausted rider. Finally they approached a heavy clump of cottonwood and willow saplings, growing low to the ground. The horse stood patiently at the edge of the tangle. The dog growled several times at the sleeping rider, but still Luke slept on.

Impatiently the dog woofed more loudly, scuffing his feet, his eyes glowing in the dark. Then he gave a sharp warning bark, and Luke stirred in the saddle.

He took in the bunch of trees, and said to the dog: 'Good boy! It's time we rested, eh?'

With an effort he dismounted, and led Blazer into the tangle of trees and brush. He tethered the horse to the bushes and cut some willow branches with his bowie knife. Then once again he went out onto the prairie where he backtracked the horse a considerable distance. Exhausted, he swept the tracks of horse and dog out of the dust with the leafy branches. Fortunately, the horse had been following a well-traveled trail when he had branched off for the trees, and there were plenty of tracks to confuse anyone on his trail.

Back in the trees he made sure of the hitch on the bridle but he did not dare unsaddle the horse. He picked out a level spot on the ground and fell at once into a sleep of deep exhaustion. The dog sat beside him, and finally rested his head on his paws and listened as Luke began to snore. For perhaps a quarter of an hour the animal remained thus, then he stealthily raised up and stole away, moving carefully and leaving scarcely a track in the soft sand.

★   ★   ★

Back at the rim of the gorge the separated elements of Morgan's posse had at last gotten together. True, it was only after the larger body had made one more glorious start behind the wavering, howling dog pack—only to stop, exasperated, when the dogs came upon the three lounging guards.

Now a huge fire burned at the rim of the canyon. Other men held flaming torches aloft, making the whole scene a tremendous stage upon which Honest John Morgan paced back and forth. About a hundred feet back from the edge, the forty-odd horses stood tethered to a long line run from some rocks. A half-dozen men stood near the horses, keeping them quiet and the lines untangled. Standing apart from everyone else were three men—Tex, the man

134

called Earl, and their luckless companion. Around them in a huge semicircle sat the gang of riders. They were a hardened lot and the look of them, with the firelight on their faces, was ugly indeed. They had all ridden for Morgan before, and now they realized the seriousness of the chief's mood.

Morgan, between the fire and the rim, had cast off his coat. His black hair, streaked with white, was rumpled and mussed.

He looked up at the circle of men. 'If we're ready Ace, we'll start.'

'We're ready, Jack,' answered the lieutenant. 'They've got the dogs leashed.'

'These three men—' Morgan paused. 'These three'—he let the impact of his revulsion sink in on the trio—'they stood there, and let those two dirty, foul rats sneak by them!'

He cleared his throat and continued: 'Not sneak by on their bellies, like the snakes that they are, but let them *walk* right by, leading their horses with them. And leading *my* white horse!'

He turned to the solitary figure standing at the very edge of the deep gorge. Pop Winters stood in his buckskin garments, white hair swept back in the night breeze, arms folded—a magnificent figure of a man, with the firelight dancing on his leather-smooth skin.

Morgan added; 'Winters has shown you the marks on the rock, and told you what happened. You heard from their own lips how they let them pass by.' Morgan's voice cracked, as if he were stunned by the incredulity of the thing. 'How they even *talked* to them, and let them bluff their way through.'

'My God, Jack—Mr. Morgan—we didn't—' ventured the cowboy named Earl.

'That's right,' said Morgan, his voice a low snarl, 'you *didn't*—and that's why you're on trial here! You others have heard the story. I vote guilty. Who votes with me?'

'Guilty!' came the chorus.

'Who says Not Guilty?'

Silence fell. Pop Winters walked from the edge of the canyon away from the condemned group. Morgan sauntered to the circle of men. The three faced up to their judgment. Earl, on his knees, was praying steadily in a low voice, confessing his long list of sins.

The other man seemed stunned; he stood listlessly, head bowed, hands hanging lax at his sides.

Tex had not made excuses. Now the lean, mean-looking cowpuncher slunk toward the lip of the gorge, hands resting on the two Colt butts, like large hip bones at his skinny waist. A curse was on his lips for Jack Morgan and all his crew; he prepared to die as he had lived—violently.

The execution would be simple. All forty would draw and shoot at once at the signal.

136

Thus, no man could be sure whose bullet had taken a life. It was the custom at these trials not to disarm the prisoners, for in the face of such odds, firearms were of no practical use. Then, too, there were a dozen good men with Winchesters nearby.

Now the signal came. Morgan raised his left hand slightly as his right darted to the small shoulder holster beneath his left arm. The fusilade of bullets tore the trio from life as each man in Morgan's pack opened up on the human target that he had selected.

Tex staggered backward, his thin body writhing and twisting in the death agony as bullet after bullet struck home. Both his guns were firing as he slanted backward off the rim. At least one of the jury would never ride again, and would soon be judged himself!

The two corpses that had died without a fight were quickly dumped off the rim to join their partner in the river.

'Tex died mean,' summed up the opinion of men, as they blew smoke from their Colts and stuffed fresh shells into the cylinders.

★   ★   ★

The first light of dawn was beginning to creep into the sky as the horsemen mounted. Morgan dashed about the scene on the huge hunter, getting the group together and shouting instructions. Now he dashed off towards Pop Winters and Ace Dawson, sitting their horses near Bob Griswold and his dog pack. He reined up before the little group.

'Are you ready to go, Griswold?'

'Yes, damn it, Jack, I'm ready. An' if I find that damn dog, I'll starve him for a week!'

'The big white wolf-dog ran off,' declared Ace Dawson.

'I'll kill the lob-eared, mangy cur—eat my meat and run off, will he! I'll poison it next time, the dirty, wild—' He broke off into a string of curses that his years among the wild, savage dogs had taught him.

Pop Winters sat his horse, calmly regarding old Bob Griswold. Although they were of the same age, the two men were a contrast in appearance. Griswold was gnarled, bent at the shoulders, his hair a dirty gray, and his pale skin blotched with red. His clothes were shabby, his face wrinkled with scorn.

Winters sat silently watching Griswold, a faint smile playing about the corners of his mouth. He was straight of back, his skin smooth, brown and unwrinkled; his hair pure white. Long ago he was, no doubt, a tall, handsome blond youth. Somehow he had come through a long life of lawlessness unmarked and unstooped. From his straight back, one might say that there sat a man of thirty-five.

'We don't need the big dog, do we,

Griswold?' asked Morgan.

'No. Hell, no! We don't need him!' Griswold shouted angrily.

But there was that quality in his voice which puzzled Morgan and Winters. It sounded as if the old man wasn't quite sure. At any rate, it was obvious even to Ace Dawson that something about the dog's disappearance worried the pack-keeper more than it should have. There was no doubt that these men attached a significance to Diablo's disappearance more than any of them was willing to admit. None of them was used to defeat, and the circumstances under which Luke and Abe had escaped annoyed them all.

The dogs were slowly unleashed from a heavy chain that ran between them. Immediately they began milling about, howling and sniffing here and there among the rocks. Griswold produced the bit of clothing from Luke's saddle pack and gave them the scent. The dogs started off in a great circle, howling and baying, while the riders waited for Griswold to gather up the leashes and chain. By the time the old man was ready, the dogs had picked up their first scent, and soon they were off in a bee line, following the trail where Luke and Abe had walked their horses.

Morgan stood in the stirrups and waved the horsemen to follow. The riders moved out in a long column of threes, with Griswold slightly in the front and shouting to the dogs by name. Behind him came Morgan, flanked by Winters and Dawson. They moved on like this for perhaps an hour; the pace was slow as the dogs worked the trail and Griswold worked the pack, shouting and hollering.

'Hey, there, you Blackie—get the hell back here! Come on now—damn those rabbits. Hey Sarge, get away from that dead carcass! Damn it, Billy, will ya quit laggin', what the hell's the matter with ya? Ya dog-gone loafer, Ned, get up here! Come on, Butch, ya yellow, mangy mutt, get in the thing, will ya—do ya want some of the whip?'

All the while he reined his horse this way and that, worrying that the dogs would take off on some animal scent and leave the pack. 'That's it, Champ—good boy! Come on, you dumb mutts get up there on the ridge with Champ—he's got more nose than the pack of ya!'

The dogs followed the great Champ up over the ridge and out of sight. The riders continued to follow the base of the ridge, as there was an easy spot to make the ascent about two hundred yards farther up the trail. They had covered perhaps half of this distance when the excited cries of the dogs reached them.

The horsemen cursed as they spurred for the spot ahead. The snarls, growls and sharp yelps carried their way by the wind were terrifying.

The dogs had either come upon a grizzly or the two fugitives themselves. Jack Morgan burst up the slope at fantastic speed, taking the lead. He urged the agile brown hunter with spur and quirt, taxing the heart of the animal as he forced it up the steep incline. All was confusion behind him as the leading horses plowed dust and stones back into the faces of those that followed. Old Bob Griswold, no great handler of horses, fell back among the other riders, his horse almost out of control. Winters and Dawson steered their horses up over the ridge behind the chief.

The three leaders paused for a moment at the top, straining for some sight of the dogs, then they located the direction of the furious struggle. It came from a deep wash about two hundred yards before them and down a long, gradual slope. They spurred the horses madly down the slope, eager to get a look at what they had trapped.

A shout came from Dawson, for the dog Butch sped toward them from the wash, blood gushing from his side. The fight had lasted long enough for Butch.

CHAPTER THIRTEEN

When Diablo sneaked away from the exhausted and sleeping Luke Barnes, he had quietly worked his way back along the trail that Luke and the marshal had taken. When he came to the spot where the two had parted, he carefully zigzagged the trail, knowing in his fighting heart that his own scent would confuse and terrify the hounds that would follow. High on a nearby hill, silhouetted against the silver moon, a lone wolf let out his solitary wail. Diablo turned and stared in the direction that the howl had come from, settling back on his haunches, his tail switched slowly as he watched the wild animal.

He might have been recalling the wild life he had led for a time, living out here in the open, running at the head of a wolf pack, dominating the cunning beasts. There had been the fights of tooth and claw with wolf, coyote and mountain lion. That was a life where all that mattered was that others retreated before his snarl and curled lip. The joy of the hunt, the sudden dash upon the victim; teeth locking in struggling flesh. The joy of the conflict with the savage, fighting males for a wild mate that would fight you tooth and claw after you had won her!

He watched the wolf for a long time, but then

142

he remembered the man back in the tangle of trees, and he rose and trotted down the trail toward the approaching chorus of the dog pack. He could sense something about the man back there that somehow made them akin. He hated mankind, yet back in the foggy past there was memory of kindness; when he was a puppy he had known that.

As he had grown into his shaggy, ferocious maturity, men had grown to fear him. Running wild as he was, there were few who would venture close; instead most would throw a rock or pick up a stick if he wandered near. Then he had been caught in the cruel trap set by Griswold, and starved into obedience. After that he hated man more than ever, but obeyed out of fear of Griswold's savage taming methods.

When he had faced Luke in that moment of truth before springing at his throat, he had sensed the difference in the man and he knew the feeling of friendship for the first time since the long-distant past. The man had petted him and spoken to him affectionately; affection made him feel different than he had ever felt. Now he was hurrying forward to fight for his friend.

Craftily he chose his battlefield in a deep dry wash among a group of large boulders. He laid a wily trail from the tracks of the marshal and Luke—a trail leading straight to this nest of

143

huge boulders. Finally satisfied, he went to a spot in ths shadows between two large rocks and lay down to wait, all senses sharply alert.

He heard the bragging yell of the dog called Champ and his lip curled; he could easily split Champ's throat and let out that boastful howl. Now came the constant baying of the bloodhound King; one slash of his mighty paw with the great sharp claws extended would silence that sad-eyed coward!

There was the bark of foolish Blackie, sounding as if he was chasing a lowly rabbit again. He strained the sensitive, pointed ear forward trying to recognize others in the chorus of howls that was growing closer. Instinctively, he knew that death was near; he could ruin the pack, but he knew also the viciousness of the killers running this way. They would ring him, of course, and though he made them pay dearly, some cur could still dart in from behind and hamstring him. Then, crippled in the hindquarters, he would have to drag himself through the fight. He could fight until one of the pack got a grip on his neck from behind; then he would feel the bones and nerves of his spine crunch together, and the end would be near.

Now his eyes shone with the wild joy of battle as the red sun rose. The dog Champ topped the rise above the wash and with a howl plunged down. Two more of the pack followed. Diablo's

144

belly came off the ground as he rose slowly on his legs, watching the three dogs shuffle about, noses to the ground.

Then the great gray hound called Champ looked up and locked eyes with the waiting wolf-dog. For perhaps a fraction of a second he hesitated, then his feet cleared the ground and with a savage roar he flung himself at Diablo's throat. While he acted quickly, he was the more surprised of the two, for during that first flying somersault, his throat had been torn loose from his neck. When he landed he was Champ no longer, but only a convulsing heap of dying tissue.

The other two dogs had flown to the attack. The large bloodhound called King was swiftly dispatched with a severed hind leg hanging by threads. The other dog, a vicious fighter named Jackie, clung tenaciously to a fold of skin on Diablo's back, his jaws locked as the great dog strove to throw him off. Then the hold was loosened with a cry of pain as Diablo's razor-sharp teeth ground through his hind leg.

The ten other dogs cleared the edge of the wash in a heap and landed on the white bundle of fury. Like a huge, snarling, multicolored bear, the mass of dogs rolled and pitched. Suddenly out of the ball of bloody fur thrust the head and shoulders of the white dog and locked in his jaws was a smaller hound. This hound the white dog shook as a man might shake a dirty rag, to fling the dog back over his head, its neck broken.

Then the white dog was down in the pack in the savage battle, rolling about the floor of the dry wash, the cries of pain and snarls of hatred mingling together. At that point the dog called Butch raced from the fray out of the wash and up the hill. And the white dog stood alone, panting, tongue hanging out, head down. There were two other dogs obviously alive but use of their hind legs was lost to them. They sat panting heavily, regarding the bloody white dog. Then, hearing the approach of horses, Diablo slowly began a weary trot up the dry wash, away from the approaching men.

He was bleeding from two dozen wounds, but he held his head up and increased his speed as he dashed along the dry, twisting stream bed. He knew that he must be far away when the wounds began to stiffen him, and the faster he ran now, the longer this would take. His fights with the wild things in the past had taught him this, and it saved him now. He came out of the dry wash about the same time the forty horsemen cantered down into the site of the battle. He was away and free, running strongly toward the hiding place where he'd left Luke. There would be no more trailing with the dogs.

Morgan and the others could scarcely believe their eyes when they came upon the scene, for there in the sunrise lay ten dead or dying dogs.

The three that would live were badly maimed. They might make some child a good pet, but their fighting days had ended, and the fear that showed in their eyes was proof of this. Bob Griswold strode among the dogs, alternately cursing and crying, vowing that he would not rest until he caught the kill-crazed lion or bear that had done this.

The men, tired from the long night of riding without rest, silently followed Morgan back toward Denver. Some slept as they jogged along the trail, others talked in low tones about the strange happenings. Morgan rode alone and in bad temper, and Griswold had stayed behind, trying to help his three surviving dogs.

Luke awoke from his long sleep and looked into the eyes of Diablo, for the dog sat with his head close to Luke's face. As Luke stirred, the tail began to wag and the dog focused his attention on the face of his friend. Luke stretched and rolling onto his side, reached to pat the dog, startled when he saw the red and brown stains of caked blood.

'What happened, boy?' Luke asked, rising to his knees and examining the wounds. He looked about for signs of a struggle. Diablo lay still, looking up at his new friend and playing for sympathy by giving a low whine.

'What's that, feller? Hurts does it? Here, let Luke have a look again.'

The big dog let the man roll him about on the

ground, examining the wounds. After careful inspection, Luke decided that, despite the dog's many fearsome gashes and tears, he was not mortally hurt.

He patted Diablo and said: 'What was it boy, mountain lion or bear?'

Luke considered that he hadn't had any food since he had left Rielly's. It was now late in the following afternoon, and his stomach had that old gnawing feeling. He checked the Colt on his hip and walked off into the wooded area. Diablo bounded to his side, running a little stiff-legged, but still running.

As they approached a serviceberry bush, a large jackrabbit exploded from its base. Luke slung the Colt into line and was about to take his lead on the jack and fire when the white dog bounded in. Four big leaps and he came down with both paws on the rabbit's backbone. The dog carefully put his mouth around the head and squeezed down. Luke heard the bones crunch.

'Good hunter!' praised Luke, walking to the animal and reaching for the prize. 'Pretty fast jumpin' for a cripple.'

But the dog, with his mouth around the rabbit's head, answered with a series of warning growls.

'Oh, so that's the way you want it, eh?' Luke nodded, backing off. 'I guess I can catch my own, anyway!'

Luke walked on. The dog watched him go and as soon as he was sure that his kill wasn't going to be challenged, he picked it up and trotted after Luke. They moved along for a while, poking here and there at the thicker bushes when suddenly another rabbit burst from cover. Luke wasted no time now, and the rabbit cartwheeled with the crash of the Colt. Luke turned and looked at the dog and walked to his kill; the dog watching with interest as he picked it up.

'Come on, boy,' said Luke. 'We're goin' to breakfast!'

They walked back to the spot where he had slept. He talked to the horse for the first time that day and made that fine animal more comfortable by removing the saddle. Taking the rope he shook it out and fashioned a crude hackamore, giving Blazer some slack so that he could graze more easily.

Next he gathered a pile of dry twigs and started a little blaze going, adding a few larger sticks to build up a fine smokeless blaze. Through all of this Diablo had been carefully chewing the feet from the rabbit. This was his usual procedure, since he had long ago become convinced that when the game he captured disappeared, it had come to life and run off. It seemed never to occur to him that some other predatory animal might have had the audacity to steal it from him.

Luke took his knife from its sheath and tested the edge with his thumb. He flopped the limp rabbit onto the log beside him and quickly lopped off the feet. He made a slit up from the belly and gutted the carcass, and two more cuts down the hind legs. Then, with the skill that comes of long practice, he snapped the skin off the carcass and cut through the neck with one incision of the heavy blade. He held the neatly skinned carcass aloft for the dog to behold.

'Now there's a tasty dish, Diablo. No fur to stick in your throat; all meat, and just a little bone.'

The insides he wrapped in the pelt and buried the whole lot in a scooped-out hole nearby. Next, he cut two forked sticks and forced them into the ground near the fire. He whittled a long pointed stick to skewer the rabbit, and set the animal roasting over the fire.

As the first aroma of the roasting meat drifted about the clearing, Diablo's head came erect. The dog gently tasted the air with his nose and for the first time he seemed interested in Luke's rabbit. He dropped his own animal across his front paws, and watched as Luke turned the cooking rabbit on the spit, with the juices bubbling out, building up a delicious crust.

Luke cut a long strip of meat from the flank and tossed it in the air to the dog, hearing the jaws snap shut with a crack. He cut a piece of meat for himself and smacked his lips at the good flavor, then sliced another for the dog, and so on until only some bones remained. The meat was dry and they had no salt or water, but the hunger pains were gone when they had finished.

After the meal, Luke began his preparations for the ride into Denver, while Diablo licked at the sores he had acquired early that morning. First, Luke took all the cartridges from the ornately engraved Colt and spun the cylinder a few times. Next he dry-fired the gun at objects about the clearing: here a stick, there a rock.

He was not completely satisfied with the operation of the main spring, so he removed the carved walnut grips from the frame. He took out the small whittled block of wood that was wedged inside the handle, tightly cramping the spring. It was the first thing he had done to the gun upon returning to his room the day the remainder of the Sundown Gang had jumped him. It was an old trick among gunsmiths in setting a hair trigger.

The hammer was cocked just that much easier; the time that it saved could only be measured in fractions of a single second, yet it could be the difference between life and death. He cut another piece of wood and cramped the spring still more; then reassembled the grip and tried the hammer again. Now satisfied, he loaded the gun and holstered it.

The heavy-bladed knife now occupied his

attention. From a slit in the sheath he extracted a small, thin file of fine German steel. With this tool he scraped at the already-keen edge. Finally he put the file away and produced from a pocket a small whetstone. Spitting on this, he honed the knife for a while, working the small stone up and down the blade. He finished the job by stropping the edge on his leather boot.

Luke took a small square of metal from his wallet and smoothed some of the dents from the surface. It was a poor mirror, and the reflection that looked back at him from it was that of a heavy-bearded desperado, if ever he saw one! He thought of Rielly, and without hesitating he began to hack away at the whiskers. It was slow and painful work without water or lather, but the knife was as sharp as any barber's razor, and when he finished the shave was fairly close and complete. Of course, he knicked himself, but he was more pleased with the reflection that now gazed up from the tin mirror.

Next, he saddled up the big white, kicked sand over the fire and turned to the dog.

'Let's go fella. We've a long way to go and a lot to do!'

He swung into the saddle and headed out of the trees at a brisk trot. The dog came along, slightly stiff from his hurts. It was the first time he had held the big white to a trot and he was pleased with the gait, for the hoofs scarcely seemed to touch the ground. They kept moving all through the early evening, the big horse easily carrying the rider, and the dog trotting along behind.

It was after dark when Luke reined in the horse behind a building on the edge of town. He hobbled the horse with the long reins and crept down the narrow space between two of the buildings. As he approached the street side of the buildings the sound of voices brought him to a halt. He held the dog by the scruff of the collar and then quietly crept closer to the mouth of the alley.

Pressed against the wall, he watched two men who were speaking in low tones. The light from the windows across the street dimly illuminated the scene. The one man was tall and thin, dressed like the ordinary cowpuncher and the other might have been a merchant or storekeeper. This man was short and stout, but with amazingly long arms. He was attired in a large black coat of good quality, and on his head sat a white ten-gallon hat.

The clothing of the second man jogged Luke's memory, and a daring plan began to form in his mind; a plan that might help him to get close to Rielly without being discovered.

The heavy man spoke: 'Cost Morgan two thousand? Hell, I guess it did. Those nine horses was all thoroughbred stock, an' the ten dogs was worth somethin' to old Bob. If I know old Bob, he'll get his pay all right.'

'I guess he *got* his pay, Frank.'

The other nodded and said: '*Four* was killed I guess; them that come back was a little tight-lipped about the whole thing.'

'Well, I heard from young Bill Horn that the two of 'em jumped their horses across a twenty-foot ravine! Bill said he checked the drop, an' it was two hundred feet. Bill said they'd be dead now if they hadn't had the two best hosses in the county!'

'Morgan paid a thousand for the white stallion,' confirmed the stout man.

'I guess they still had a chance to run 'em down until the dogs stumbled into a army of mountain lions havin' a convention, or somethin',' said the thin man.

'Well, Chick, those dogs took care of a lot of lions in their day, so I guess they ended up about even, eh? Personally, I was glad to hear that the big white dog ran off. I never did like the sight of the ugly brute,' said fat Frank.

By some unexplained coincidence this last remark brought a very low growl from the dog beneath Luke's hand. Luke shook the dog's head gently for silence.

'What was that?' asked Frank. 'Didja hear that little rumble?'

'My stomach,' burped the thin man. 'I just finished a powerful big load of ham an' cabbage.'

'For a minute it sounded just like a dog

growlin',' said the heavyset man, much relieved. 'How about a little night cap over at Flynn's Saloon, Chick?'

'No thanks, Frank, I'm turnin' in early,' replied the man named Chick. They exchanged good nights, and Chick headed up the street, whistling as he went.

★ ★ ★

The stout man, Frank, turned in the other direction. As he came to the opening between the buildings, a long, muscular arm darted from the opening and powerful fingers hooked the collar of the man's coat. He came flying backward into the alley, where Luke spun him around and threw him against the opposite wall.

Frank was not the type of man who liked the dark; in fact, he usually avoided the streets after sundown. Now, as he sagged against the wall, his knees were knocking and his heart pounding. He gazed into the eyes of his captor who held him there, the great fist bunching his shirt just below his throat, while the veritable saber in the other hand pricked his Adam's apple. At that moment he was sure that another monster had firmly taken his hand in its teeth!

'Hello, Frank,' said the captor. 'I'm gonna buy your coat an' hat.'

'Th-th-that's okay,' stammered Frank.

'How much did you pay, Frank?'

'Fi-fi-fifty bucks.'

'Sold.' Luke peeled the coat from the man's back and lifted the hat from his head. He placed the hat on his own head and stepped back to try on the coat. As Luke did so, the dog released his grip on the man's hand and stood on his hind legs with his paws on Frank's shoulders. The huge animal forced his hundred and thirty pounds against the man's sagging frame and curled his lips back, revealing long rows of glistening white teeth. Diablo accompanied his friendly smile with a low snarl, and Frank moaned in fright.

'He's just tryin' to be friendly,' explained Luke, chuckling. 'Okay, Frank. The coat fits good. Here's a hundred dollars.' Luke pressed the two fifties into the fat, sweating hand. 'Fifty for the clothes, and fifty to forget that you saw us here.'

'I'm dreamin' I saw you, mister. My Gawd, make him get down, will ya please?'

'I'll make him get down. But just *one* word about our little transaction here tonight, and I'll let him have you for breakfast. Savvy?'

'My Gawd—I sure do!'

'Come Devil, baby,' called Luke as he retreated down the alley.

'M-my Gawd—"*baby*," he said!' Frank muttered, aghast.

The dog dropped down and slunk up the alley disappearing in the gloom after the figure of the man who led him.

Luke mounted Blazer with a new respect; never had he been so expensively horsed. He brought the animal around one of the side streets and stepped along at a brisk trot, the dog pacing behind, sniffing at the strange town smells. Luke pulled the wide brim of the ten-gallon hat down over his eyes and gathered the coat about him. The coat was a surprisingly good fit, due to Frank's long arms.

As Luke came along he saw an old timer sitting on the porch of one of the lamp-lighted houses. He rode past, and the old timer called out:

'Howdy, Mr. Morgan. See you got your horse back.'

Luke touched his hand to the brim of the hat as he had seen Jack Morgan do. The gesture seemed to satisfy the old fellow, who rocked on as Luke rode by. The old man did not see the dog lope by seconds later because of the hedge and picket fence between them. Luke wished that Abe Leach could see him at that moment, parading boldly down the street, impersonating none other than Honest John Morgan. He headed the white for Jake Kearns' street and cut around in back of the restaurant. He tied the horse in the small fenced-in yard.

Luke knocked on the rear door, and in a few seconds Jake Kearns' big figure filled the opening, light from the kitchen shining behind him. 'Why, Mr. Morg—Well, I'll be damned, Luke Barnes, *himself*!' Jake grinned all over. 'Come in boy, come in with ya.'

Luke entered, and Jake closed the door. 'What can I do for ya, my boy?'

'Feed me,' said Luke. 'I'm so hungry I could eat a horse, and if horse-eating is a crime, I'd sure hang—because that's a stolen horse out there.'

'I'd know that horse anywhere, but I got to admire ya for what ya done and the odds ya been buckin'. That's swingin' people your way. They're sayin' that if you an' Abe Leach didn't have somethin' pretty good on Morgan, you'd both light out for the border. But you two been a-hangin' onto the fight, buckin' the greatest odds this town has ever seen.'

As he talked, he poured a steaming mug of coffee and watched Luke swig down the liquid. He heaped a pile of stew on a plate and pushed it toward Luke who began to eat at once. Then something scratched at his back door, and a low growl filtered into the room.

'Open the door,' said Luke, 'it's all right—he won't hurt you.'

'*He*—?' asked Kearns. He swung the door open and gasped as the great dog calmly walked in, shifting his head this way and that, looking over the scene.

'He's my friend,' Luke explained with a wave of his fork. 'Give him a bone or somethin'.'

'Boy, you sure have got yourself some strange friends! First you was friends with Morgan and the rest, then you're friends with that cantankerous old Abe Leach, and now you turn up with a wild wolf. Well, okay, I got a bone that he might like to play with. He sure looks like the playful type, the way he's all covered with blood and sores.'

After making his observations, Jake grabbed a huge leg bone from his chopping block. He seemed also to find it handy to pick up his cleaver at that moment. The bone he tossed to the dog, but the cleaver he apparently had use for, and this he kept as he walked about the room, gesticulating with one hand and one cleaver.

'This friend of yours *could* have been the whole passel of mountain lions that was supposed to have hit Griswold's pack last night.' Jake winced as the dog's teeth snapped through a thick piece of the meaty bone. 'There, did ya hear that? Did ya hear the way he snapped through that steer's leg?'

'Something happened to the dogs last night?' asked Luke innocently, around a big mouthful of stew.

'*Somethin' happen*, he says! Only the whole damn pack was set on an' killed. Those that come back from your little chase said the dogs musta run into a whole army of mountain lions, with a good general to lead 'em. But this here

159

friend of yours coulda been the army and the general. For one thing, ya ever know a lion to stand and fight a pack of dogs when he could run?'

'Nope,' volunteered Luke, draining his coffee. 'And I never knew lions to fight in a group, 'cept maybe a mate will come to help its partner.'

'That's exactly it! They're cowardly around dogs and they'd all run off in different directions. But whatever got to those dogs sure didn't run. And when ya take one look at this dog and the way he's scarred up, ya got to think that he coulda played the hand.'

'That's it, of course. The dog was all right when I fell asleep around dawn this mornin'. He musta slipped back and jumped the pack. Now, *there's* a fight I'd like to have seen!'

'Here, boy, have a hunk of this beef.' Jake's eyes were shining as he tossed a two-pound chunk of sirloin to the dog. 'I never was one for huntin' men with dogs.' Jake beamed down on Diablo as he held the piece of meat in his paws and ripped off large hunks.

'Luke, your horse is in the lot behind the livery stable, along with the marshal's.'

'Thanks, Jake, but I got me a good mount for the time being. And I'd like to leave him in your yard for about a half an hour, while I take care of some other business.'

'Don't let that other business take care of

you,' warned Jake, looking seriously at his friend.

Luke and the dog slipped out the back door and headed for the rear entrance of Rielly's Saloon on foot. The patio was not guarded, and they entered, with Luke pausing to be sure that they had not been observed. Then he headed for the stone in the patio surface that led to the underground passage. He lifted the large flagstone and climbed down. The dog attempted to follow, but Luke told him to wait.

The dog sat down by the stone, seeming to understand. After Luke replaced the stone, the dog wiggled to a position over it, where he lay and waited.

Inside the passage Luke felt his way in the darkness. As he groped his way forward he expected that he would suddenly touch something ahead of him. For tonight something was probing at his sixth sense; something sinister and evil, and he could not understand the feeling.

Many times in the past he had been saved by this strong perception. Now he hesitated in the passage and concentrated on the unseen danger that he felt was ahead.

Slowly he dropped to his hands and knees, taking a full two minutes to accomplish this quiet change of position. He knew that the slightest rustling of his clothes or creaking of a joint could bring death. With the tips of his fingers he worked his way along the floor, feeling for the depressions made by those that had recently used the passage. After about ten feet he found a heelmark that was familiar, and he ran his index finger around the depression. There was a little corner protruding from one side of the mark. Remembering the notch in the heel of his boot, he knew that this track was one of his own prints that he had made the night before. Soon he located two of Abe Leach's prints, with the large flat heel that the lawman preferred. Then he felt something different, a depression he could not identify.

Exasperated, he straightened up for a second and let his hand drop to his knee. His knee—that was it! They were the depressions of a man's knee. Someone had crawled this way earlier, for the knee print had blotted out half of one of Luke's prints of the night before.

Luke paused. His sixth sense was not tricking him, then. There *was* someone here in the tunnel, perhaps just ahead of him. He sat perfectly still and stopped breathing, his ears alert. But not the faintest sound came to him. At last, he took a deep, quiet breath, trying to pick up the scent of the other. He smelled horse and he smelled campfire; these in themselves were not distinctive. But then another odor kept coming to him. Skins! Yes, it was the scent from some type of hide—and a wet hide, at that!

Luke inched along cautiously, feeling the knee prints of the man ahead. The prints still went forward. It was possible, then, that the man didn't know that Luke was there. It was possible, indeed, that he had passed well ahead. Then Luke felt a different substance in the sand. It was flat, smooth and soft, almost like grease. He picked it up and rolled it about in his fingers; it was the size of a small coin. He squeezed it, then tentatively he tasted it. It was candle wax. Someone had crawled through here, all right—but the stranger had had light. Candle light!

CHAPTER FOURTEEN

When Abe Leach left Luke he headed straight for the Howard ranch. About the time that Luke had gone to sleep, Abe was making himself a dry camp in the hills overlooking the spread. He staked the horse out to graze and found a spot where he could lie and keep the house under observation.

Breakfast smoke was coming from the chimney. Presently the slam of the cabin door came up to him and he quickly focused his gaze on the ranch yard. Halfway between the house and the pump strode Red Calhoun, a bucket swinging in one hand and a Winchester in the other.

The redhead filled the bucket and started back for the house. As he did so, he scanned the hills ringing the cabin. Suddenly, he spotted a hawk circling in the sky. He held the rifle in both hands and gazed toward the spot where Abe Leach was concealed. Finally he seemed satisfied that the hawk had sighted some harmless creature.

He picked up the bucket and headed for the cabin door. Just as he approached the porch a small figure darted from the door, but a long arm shot out of the opening and dragged the youngster back.

Abe's heart leaped at the sight of the boy, and the arm. The boy must be one of the Howard children, and the arm—he was sure—belonged to Mrs. Howard. Then, at least they were alive. Leach's face in human nature was momentarily restored. From the first he had refused to believe that range-bred men, such as those that followed Morgan, would stoop to killing a woman and her children.

He pondered how he might get close enough to the building to surprise Red. Patiently he watched the house through the day, and as the sun set he started to Injun down out of the hills.

During the day Red had chopped wood, looked to his horse in the corral and spent most of the time sitting on the porch—always with his rifle close by and his Colt strapped to his waist. He was, obviously, guarding prisoners within the cabin.

It was dark when Abe crawled to a spot near one of the windows. He cautiously rose and stared inside. The scene there seemed normal enough; the whole Howard family was there and the setting looked friendly. However, Abe noted the strain on the faces of the parents, who apparently had been cooped up like this to satisfy anyone who might come near the place.

Abe strained to overhear the conversation, and heard the man say: 'How long we goin' to be penned up like this?'

'Only till Jack says to let you loose,' replied the redhead sitting down to the supper table.

'What's the meaning of it all?' moaned the mother. 'Oh, dear, what will become of us?'

'There, there, ma'am; everything will be all right. You'll see,' Red tried to reassure the woman.

At this point a rider came pelting down out of the hills from the direction of the Denver trail. Straight to the ranch house he galloped the horse.

Abe flattened himself against the wall in the shadows.

The rider jumped down, led the animal into the corral where he gave the horse a slap, and then closed the gate.

Red Calhoun came to the front door and called: 'That you, Ben?'

'Yeah, it's me,' answered the horseman, entering the room and plunking down at the table. Mrs. Howard busied herself getting some food for the man.

'How are things goin' in town?' asked Red.

'Not so good,' said Ben, raising his eyebrows. The man's facial expression conveyed far more to Red than anything that had been said so far, and he was noticeably more interested in his confederate now. He looked hard at the rider and said:

'Did they—uh—did they get those two wild hosses rounded up?'

'What?' frowned Ben. 'Oh—the two *hosses!* No, they didn't. The hosses got clean away!'

Red frowned. 'You don't say!'

'I do say—an' what's more they took two good hosses with them! Morgan's Blazer and Rielly's big chestnut, Sonny.'

'Is that a fact,' said Red winking. 'Well, that's the way of wild hosses—when they make a raid they always run off with the cream of the herd.'

Calhoun paused to note the effect of the past conversation on the listening Howard family. Then he added: 'O' course, wild hosses like that can be run down—say, with a good pack of dogs, eh?'

'Sometimes they kin, but sometimes somethin' hits those dogs powerful hard and stops 'em cold!'

'You mean a sickness?' asked Red, looking up suddenly.

'This sickness strikes like chain lightnin' an' leaves 'em dead, quick! I see it, an' it wasn't pretty.'

'What caused it?'

'Could a been ten mountain lions—or maybe three bears, stirred up an' ornery.'

'Nope. Mountain lions don't bunch up like that. An' there ain't been three bear killed around here in the last four years!'

'Yeah. That's what Mr. Morgan said.'

'I thought Morgan would send the Mexican out,' said Red, frowning at the other man. The word that Ben had brought obviously did not set well with Red. It was plain that he held the whole thing against Ben, as the bearer of bad news.

'So did I, but those wild hosses kind of stepped in and fouled up the plan.'

'The Mexican, he ain't feelin' good, eh?'

'He ain't feelin' *nothin'* since that hoss tromped on his head!'

'Well! How come a hoss could stomp old Joe? Why, Joe was born on a hoss.'

'He died under one,' said Ben, taking a noisy drink of coffee. 'An' Morgan's mad as a hornet.'

'Yeah.' Red was obviously uneasy. 'What do the people around Denver think o' this—o' the two wild hosses, an' all?'

167

'Most of 'em think it's a damn funny business, what with Boom-Boom goin' down the trail, an' the Mexican cashin' in his chips.' Ben stared at the redhead and continued: 'Ace Dawson's a-talkin' to himself and Pop Winters is sulkin' around, sneakin' up on everybody.'

'Pop can generally find a trail before it's made.'

'Just the same, I don't like him sneakin' around. It gives me the creeps.'

'What was—didja hear that noise?' Red held up his hand for silence.

'What did it sound like?'

'Sounded like somethin' hit the bucket out there.' Red pushed back his chair, grabbing his rifle as he rose.

★   ★   ★

Red flung open the door and peered out into the moonlight. Ben drew his pistol and started to back Red's play. The Howards shepherded their brood into a corner of the room.

The back door creaked slightly and as Calhoun spun around, Abe Leach stood framed in the doorway, a Colt in either hand and a wooden bucket firmly wedged on one foot.

'What—?' yelled Red.

'Easy now, Red! Don't do anything that one o' these Colts might make yuh sorry fer,' said the marshal.

'He's got the drop, Red. Better do as he says,' said Ben, dropping his pistol to the floor.

'Come on, Red,' urged the marshal. 'Tip that rifle barrel up a quarter o' an inch more, will yuh? I'm sort o' put out the way things have been goin' lately; I'd kinda like to take it out on somebody.'

'Ben, you damn fool, if yuh hadn't dropped yore gun we'd a got 'em!' Calhoun snarled. Still frozen in his tracks, his pale blue eyes locked with those of Leach.

'You can talk, but one of those Colts was lookin' right at my belt buckle!' offered Ben, as an excuse for his quick surrender.

Calhoun made a face of disgust at the other, but never took his fiery eyes from those of the marshal. 'I've faced a pistol barrel twenty times Ben, an' I never been tagged by a slug yet!' Red bragged, the excitement of the coming kill working up into his face.

'There's a first time fer everythin'—Pinky!' taunted the lawman.

'*Pinky*! "Pinky" yuh call me, eh?' roared the redhead. 'We'll see who's pink, you dirty old rat! We'll see your damn pink insides.'

'Easy there, Freckles. Don't get to ravin' an' jerkin' so. It'll spoil yore aim every time.'

'"*Freckles*!"' screamed the half-berserk Calhoun. 'Why, you knob-eared sack of bones, I'm killin' you now—back out of here while you've got a chance!'

The marshal spat a thin stream of tobacco juice in Red's direction. 'Lay down that rifle, Pinky. I'm through playin' games. I can take yuh any time!'

The red-haired gunman knew he had to fight or back water. His complexion changed from fiery red to pale white, and his lips curled from his teeth in a snarl of rage. He jerked the rifle barrel up, and as it moved the two Colts spat flame and lead, driving him backward out of the door and onto the porch. Abe Leach bucket-footed across the room, his guns ready. A killer like Red was dangerous until the last spark of life had left his body—this Leach knew from bitter experience, and he made sure that the gunman would never kill again before he returned to the house.

One look at Ben, and Abe Leach knew that the man was a good candidate to go straight. He walked up to Ben and jammed one of the smoking muzzles into the stomach of the cowering man.

'Were ya ridin' in that little posse the other night, Benjamin?'

'Yes, sir,' Ben answered truthfully.

'I'm gonna have to hold that agin ya, Ben.'

'Yes, sir.'

'But, how'd you like to walk out o' here alive? I reckon you'd like that, eh, Ben? Well, that's what I'm gonna let ya do.'

'Marshal, I'll go straight as a bullet for the

rest of my days!'

'All right, get on your hoss and ride like hell. When you get to Denver tell the first *woman* you see that the Howard Family's all alive and safe—that they been kept holed-up here by Jack Morgan. Then go to Morgan himself and tell him that I had a little disagreement with Red Calhoun, but that Red died with an open mind about the whole thing.'

Having instructed the reformed gunman, the marshal holstered his Colts and flopped down at the table to survey his foot trouble.

Ben cleared the door at a bound, yelling his thanks and giving promises of the good works that he would do in the bright future. In no time at all he was beating his horse toward Denver.

Pete Howard gingerly cleared the porch of the late Red Calhoun, and Mrs. Howard clucked about the room, tidying up and getting a meal on the table for the marshal.

For the old lawman, it was a satisfying moment. The children crowded about him as he worked the ejector rod on the Colt to free the cylinders of the empty brass shells. He put fresh slugs into the empty chambers and then swung one of the little boys up on his lap for a chat.

All in all, it had been a rather satisfying day for Abe.

CHAPTER FIFTEEN

Luke had worked his way to the part of the passage that formed the intersection with the tunnel leading to Rielly's room. He turned up this passage quickly, and found it a series of long steps that rose through the building between two widely spaced walls.

The walls had, no doubt, been erected by the clever father of Jane Rielly; the stairs had been added later by the late saloonman, thus preserving the secret. Luke now had to duck his head to avoid an obstruction that passed straight through the passage. This obstacle, he surmised, would probably be a doorway passing through the two walls. The next obstruction blocked the passageway completely and felt like the rough masonry of a concealed chimney, humped out at the bottom, indicating the back of a fireplace. As he examined it, his knee struck a hard object, which appeared to be a heavily forged hinge. His heart leaped as he ran his hand down and felt another of the same size below it and then another below that. He moved quickly to the other side now and felt an iron bar sticking to the side. This he grasped and pulled slowly. With a groan, the masonry back of the fireplace creaked open, revealing the room within.

On the room side, the lever that he had worked was an innocent iron arm for holding a pot. He stepped through the fireplace and into the room. The hearth had been swept clean and he left no tracks. The room itself, he noted, was simply furnished and yet it was obvious that Rielly had her share of frilly luxuries. The bed was covered with a blue satin spread, the draperies were made to match, as was the thick carpet covering the floor. A dressing table and its mirror dominated one wall, the table top covered with perfumes and powders. The closet door stood ajar, revealing gowns and dresses, as well as some boyish-looking riding clothes.

He looked in the mirror and brushed cobwebs from his coat and hat, then settled down in a chair, determined to wait for Rielly or whoever came through the door. As he waited he could hear voices drifting up from the saloon below.

Sitting in the warm room had made him drowsy, and at length he began to nod. He awoke with a start at the sound of someone in the hall. The knob of the door turned.

'Oh!' said Jane Rielly.

'Hello,' Luke said, pulling off the large white hat. 'It's me—Luke.'

'I've got eyes,' Rielly answered.

'I mean—the hat and the coat. I thought—' Luke stammered.

'You don't look anything at all like Jack,' she declared.

'I'm sure glad you're all right, Rielly, ma'am.'

'Why shouldn't I be all right?'

'Well, I thought—I mean your gettin' the horses for us, and all. I thought that you—'

'Jack told me to get the horses. He wanted me to ride with him. He must have thought that the chase would thrill me. Where's the marshal? He isn't hurt, is he?'

'No. He's safe enough, too. I mean he's at the Howard ranch. Darn it all, I hope he's all right.' Luke was embarrassed, and he fumbled with the hat, trying to think of something to say.

'Don't you feel silly, running here and leaving him out there all alone?' questioned Jane with a teasing look in her eye.

Luke looked at the floor. 'Well, I—that is, I thought you might need help, and I ...' He ended lamely.

'I can take care of myself,' she answered, flouncing to the window. 'By the way, how did you manage to bite all those dogs the other day?'

'I didn't—my dog did it. I mean Diablo did it. You know Diablo, don't you?'

'Sure, we're good friends,' she teased.

'Well, he's a regular bear of a dog. He likes me—why, he chased me for hours the other night.'

174

'Sounds real friendly.'

'Well, I don't mean it that way, but darned if the ugly brute didn't take to me after he saw my face up close.'

'Sounds reasonable.'

'Oh, for heaven sakes, stop twistin' everything I say! The dog made friends with me an' then he turned on the pack. That's not so hard to believe, is it?'

'Naw,' she said, copying his vernacular. 'It happens every day.'

'Now see here, Rielly, I didn't come here to be laughed at. I—well—I never could talk worth a hang to a female, and I never cared much till now.'

This speech seemed to have some sobering effect on the girl, and she seemed to feel rather badly about the way she had been joshing him. She took a brush from the dressing table, and coming over near where he sat, she dropped to the floor before him.

'Brush my hair, Luke.'

'Oh, God!' cried Luke in helpless embarrassment.

'Go on, brush it!' she commanded.

He tried to draw the brush through the fine red-gold strands, but the brush stuck.

'Sorry; it's a lot finer than a horse's mane.'

'Thanks.'

He continued to brush her hair, at last getting the knack of it. The girl sighed, and

175

leaning her head on his knee she looked up into his face. Then she reached up and traced along his nose and around his chin with her index finger. Luke's heart pounded so loudly that he knew she must hear it thumping. He was lost in a dream of happiness.

'Luke,' she said, 'Luke, kiss me.'

She turned her head and mouth up to meet his. Their lips met in a clumsy crush at first, but they lingered. It became very sweet, and he held her head in both hands as he bent in the embrace. Presently she drew away and looked deeply into his astounded eyes.

'Luke, I love you. You're my man—you're what I've been waitin' for.'

'Oh, Rielly, I love you, too!' Luke whispered, his heart leaping. He bent and kissed her again, then stood up, his lips on fire and his brain reeling. He almost fell as he headed for the fireplace.

'Where are you going?' she cried.

'To get Morgan,' he answered.

'Wait,' she commanded, rising and coming to him. 'You can't go after him alone—he'd kill you like nothing! You're right in his camp, and you'll need Abe Leach and all the help you can get. I've seen him in action, and you can't stop him alone, Luke; go get Marshal Leach. Besides, Abe might need your help at this very instant.'

'One can go where two can't,' argued Luke.

'No. Go get the marshal; he's the law and he can help you. The Howards aren't dead; you're really not wanted by the law at all. I overheard some of the gang talking, the Howards are being held by Red Calhoun. The whole thing was a trick to get you and the marshal out of the way quickly.'

'Well, I'll be—'

'Hurry, Luke, he may need you. I've kept you here to myself long enough.' She pushed him into the fireplace. 'Good-bye, my dearest.' She blew him a kiss off her fingertips as he swung the masonry panel closed.

He fairly skipped down the passage, bumping his head twice before he slowed down; as he put out his right hand to steady himself, he brushed a flap of wood. It pivoted aside, and a slender shaft of light penetrated the darkness.

Luke stopped short and peered through the hole. The opening was about an inch in diameter. From it he could see the swinging doors of the saloon, all of the bar, most of the tables, and a great deal of the floor space. Presently he pivoted the piece of wood back into position and felt his way forward. When he came to the intersection he paused once more, sniffing the air, every sense alert to the unknown danger, of which his instinct once more was insistently warning him.

Luke sniffed the air again; the same odor of wet hide seemed strongest in the direction of the room under the bar. Slowly he inched his way forward on hands and knees, feeling the floor as he went. Suddenly, as he turned a bend, he saw a crack of light from beneath the door. Someone was in the room at that moment—probably the man of the knee prints.

Luke crept on, using ten minutes to cover the last ten feet. After much patient maneuvering he brought his eye to the crack of light.

Inside the room Pop Winters sat poised before the table, framed in the flickering candle light, his attention focused on the voices coming from above. He was obviously enjoying the ease of eavesdropping that the once-secret room afforded.

Luke jerked open the door, covering the old man with his Colt.

If Pop Winters was surprised at the intrusion there was no trace of it in his face. His smile was as cold as it always was, and as usual, there was no reflection of mirth in his eyes. He gazed steadily at Luke with a strange hypnotic stare.

'Come in! I won't hurt yuh!' said the veteran owlhooter.

Luke blinked, trying to return the cold, snake-like gaze. Then he closed the door, saying, 'Lay the hands on the table, Pop, face up. Let's see what artillery you're carryin'.'

Luke warily stepped close and began to feel about the old crook's garments for additional weapons. The big Colt he quickly stuffed in his own belt. The tight deerskin garments offered few hiding places, but Luke managed to find a double-barreled derringer in a wrist holster; a long, thin stiletto tucked away in one boot, a spring-blade knife in one of his pockets, as well as the usual sheath knife.

Luke whistled as he regarded the handful of murderous weapons. 'Pop, you're a walkin' arsenal!'

'Yo're a dead man!'

'I feel pretty lively at the moment, old timer,' said Luke, salting away the weapons on his own person.

'All I got to do is holler, an' you're trapped!'

'All I've got to do is pull this trigger, and yo're a dead, old man.'

'Pull it, if yuh got the guts. But they'll still get yuh.'

Luke made a motion with his Colt barrel at the head of the old renegade. 'I'll have to buffalo you if you don't shut up.'

Luke found some old rope on the shelf with which he bound the prisoner securely. He stepped back and looked at the bonds. Pop looked harmless enough trussed up like this, and Luke completed the job by forming a gag with the man's bandanna. He looked deeply into Winters' eyes, and believing that he read a story there, took more rope and made a noose, passing a loop over the beam above. He finished off the job by lashing the outlaw's feet to the post. It seemed to him that the old renegade would hang himself if he struggled too hard. And unless the man chewed through the gag, it looked like Pop would be out of circulation for at least two days. But the expression of mirth in Winters' eyes at that moment puzzled him.

'See you later, you salty old pelican,' said Luke with a mock salute. 'Guess you weren't as tough as the marshal had you pegged for.'

Luke closed the door, taking the candle with him. This time he went through the tunnel rapidly, and in a few minutes he was straining to raise the large flagstone cover. Diablo bumped noses with him as he hauled himself free of the hole.

He replaced the cover and crouched near the wall with the dog at his side. Some men were going by in the alley and he hesitated, waiting for them to get out of sight before making a run for his horse.

'—from the Howard ranch, eh?' one of them said.

'Yeah,' said the other. 'Ben rode in a while ago—damn near killed a horse. He said that Marshal Leach split Calhoun wide open!'

'My God, he musta bushwhacked him, then! I never seen any man quicker than Red.'

'Ben says it was a stand-off. They both had the drop, but Calhoun cracked like a woman, Ben said.'

'Well, Leach is no slouch. Why, I remember

180

the time in Leadville when—' and the voices trailed off as the men went on.

Luke heard the crunch of stone. He whirled, just as Diablo leaped with a growl. In disbelief he stared as Pop Winters seemed to come at him through the air. His face was contorted in a fierce scowl; he was actually in the middle of a leap for Luke's back, his arm was outstretched and his hand gripped a slender pin-point dagger.

Luke shouted, and grabbed for his own sheath knife. He deflected the outlaw's wrist, then got a grip on it, as did the other to his wrist. They rolled about, struggling for a chance to thrust.

Into the melee, with an excited bark, plunged Diablo, biting and clawing where he could.

With all his might, Luke tried to hold the wrist of the wily old fighter. He could see the sharp, narrow blade glimmer in the moonlight as it hung poised a scant six inches over the space between his eyes. It was the kind of needle-like knife that a strong man could drive right through a skull, or punch through a rib to the heart.

The wrist of the outlaw was heavily greased and he twisted it within Luke's grasp, trying desperately to prick the wrist of the hand that held it. Soon Luke realized that he could not hold back the seemingly eternal strength of the old man's arms. In this moment he looked into

Winters' eyes, and they were indeed the merciless eyes of a rattler.

The two men had rolled about with the knife point getting closer to Luke, while his own blade was helplessly pinioned by Winters' grip of steel. Luke strove with all his power to bring his knife home and to move the other away. With a prodigious effort, he gained a little on his adversary. Again he mustered all his strength, aiming his knife for Winters' heart, but only lost a fraction of the distance he had gained, and he knew that the struggle was lost. The tip of the knife pricked the flesh of his forehead.

It was then that Diablo got his first good grip on the outlaw's forearm. Grinding jaws scissored through skin and bones as Luke felt his hand come free. Muscular reflex made his hand spring like the jaws of a closing trap, sinking the knife past Winters' ribs and through his heart.

As the steel pierced the outlaw, the man's whole body convulsed in one tremendous nervous reaction, trying to kill even in death. Luke held on for one more second, then he rolled to the side, and the corpse of Pop Winters fell face-down.

Not until he pried the fingers of the dead outlaw's hand away from about his wrist, did Luke realize that the dog had bitten cleanly through the man's forearm. Winters' hand had been slashed free while he yet lived, and the fingers still clung in their tenacious grip.

Dazed and nauseous, Luke wanted to fall back and rest, but already the noise of the fight had carried to those who had recently passed. He could hear them shouting and running back. He staggered to his feet and stumbled out into the street, trying to make his legs move. He dashed through the space between two houses, the dog at his side, anxiously looking up at him.

'Hey—what the hell!' yelled one of the men, running into the small courtyard.

Luke paused to listen.

'It's—it's Pop Winters, gone plumb tuh hell, with only one hand!'

Luke ran on, dodging around houses, heading for Jake Kearns' and the fastest horse he had ever known. At his side ran his greatest friend.

CHAPTER SIXTEEN

Luke, taking no chances, made a zigzag dash across the remaining open ground to the fenced area behind Kearns' restaurant. Blazer gave a big snort when the man and the dog panted up. Luke snatched the reins and leaped into the saddle, then the three dashed from the yard and made a run for the open country.

183

A quarter-mile from town he drew rein and listened for sounds of pursuit. He heard none, and after a brief rest he rode around the town in a wide circle, heading for the trail toward the Howard ranch.

Presently he recognized the landmarks of the trail and he settled the horse to a steady pace. The sky had blown clear and the stars and moon showed the way.

In spite of his recent experience, he was filled with happiness at the thought of Rielly. He was glad, too, that he had met Morgan, for through the master outlaw, he had been led to Abe Leach and Jane Rielly. Thanks to Morgan he had the great horse, Blazer, at least for the present; and he vowed he would always keep the wild dog with him.

Luke's attention was brought abruptly from his thoughts by the approach of a lone rider ahead. He recognized Abe Leach on the big chestnut horse. They drew up abreast of each other.

'Howdy, son. See yuh got a new coat,' said the marshal.

'Yeah. Had a nice white hat too, but Pop Winters knocked it off,' answered Luke.

'That all Pop Winters did?'

'Well, he tried to push a little pointed dagger through my head, too, but Diablo kind of bit him, and he died on my knife, instead!'

'"Kinda" bit him, did he?' said the marshal

raising his shaggy brows and regarding the dog who sat watching them. 'I'll bet it wuz a big piece; an' tough, too! Anyhow, son, the odds is gettin' a little brighter now. The Howards is all alive and fine—the whole thing was trumped up by Morgan to give him an excuse to get us lynched. Missus Howard sent a sandwich to give yuh.' He fumbled in his saddlebag for the small package and handed it over to Luke.

'They's all nice folks, the Howards. The old man's a little crabby right now, but he's a good sort.'

Luke told him about the visit to Rielly's, leaving out certain parts, and told about the meeting with Pop Winters, after the miracle that the outlaw had performed in releasing himself from the hard-tied ropes.

'He was a great one fer that,' observed the lawman. 'Why, I remember some other fellows that tied old Pop up, and most o' them died right sudden after they tied that old tiger's tail.'

'But he couldn't have had that knife on him after I searched him!' Luke protested.

'He did, though. And he probably started cuttin' those ropes the minute you got out o' there!' Abe paused and chewed his tobacco for a while. 'Son, I'm right glad yuh got that varmint—'cause, tuh tell the truth, he's always had me plumb scared!'

Luke was eating the sandwich when Abe made this remark, and it helped to disguise his

185

expression. This admission and compliment coming as one from the old lawman touched him deeply.

'The big polecats will be startin' to get scared themselves now,' said the marshal, as though thinking aloud.

'Shall we make another try?' asked Luke.

'Yup. Only this time, let's make a *real* try at it!'

They turned the horses toward Denver and as they jogged along Luke's thoughts drifted ahead of them.

He thought of the coming battle with Jack Morgan and the reputation of ferocity that was legend concerning the fighting abilities of the outlaw boss. It was true that Morgan did not fight every day; he spent his time thinking up the clever schemes that had made him the most successful outlaw west of the Mississippi. While he did not fight often, on occasion he became involved in battle for the sheer joy of the combat. Those who had seen him were the makers of the Jack Morgan legend, and they claimed that he was a fantastic free-style fighter—not the brawling, brute-force type, but rather a crafty connoisseur of the art of defence and offence.

He was said to possess one of the finest pair of snap-shooting hands that ever practiced with a Colt. He was ambidextrous, and could shoot the spot out of an ace at twenty paces with right or left hand gun. He appeared to have two positions in a gunfight: one completely relaxed, and his hand free of the gun; the other with a gun suddenly clamped in his fist and smoke drifting from the barrel.

While he was good with a pistol of any size and doubly proficient with a rifle, it was his knowledge of knife-throwing that was truly awe-inspiring.

It was Luke's hope, as he rode along toward their destination, that they could take Morgan from either side and subdue him without a fight.

★   ★   ★

When the reformed Ben had brought his horse into Denver, it was the last hard ride that the animal would ever be called upon to make. Except as a mount for children the horse was ruined, so fast did the frightened outlaw ride.

Ben fully complied with the request of the marshal, and he told the livery-stable owner's wife and the female proprietor of a store the news about the Howard family and Red Calhoun. The news went crackling around Denver and the town was afire with the sensational story by the time Ben walked into Morgan's room.

Ben and Ace Dawson stood dumbly by as Morgan flew into a rage, pacing up and down the room, cursing and damning the marshal and Luke.

Ben slipped away during the confusion and began to make preparations for a new start elsewhere.

Ace had been shaken by the news as well, but he had managed to calm Morgan down with promises of the revenge they would reap. It had taken him an hour to calm the chief, when the men came running with the news of the strange passing of Pop Winters.

Both Morgan and Dawson stared blankly as the group of men told of their findings. Pop, who had killed upwards of half a hundred men, was gone! He had been killed—but by whom or what they were not sure; for it seemed that his arm had also been brutally bitten through.

Dawson shuddered. Although he was a man who loved to pit his strength and skill against another, he had no stomach to do battle with a man so savage as to fight in this manner. It was not the biting so much that bothered him; to deliver a good bite at the proper moment in a gouging, stomping free-for-all was a practice he had frequently followed, and it would usually break the hold of an opponent. But to gnaw through another man's limb, no matter how hated he was, was a brand of ferocity he could not comprehend. He desired no contact whatever with this half-man and half-animal.

Morgan became immediately interested in the

Pop Winters story, and in the fact that Pop was found in back of Rielly's—the very same point where the marshal and Luke had so mysteriously disappeared. Excited into action, he stripped to his shirt and leather vest, and from the closet took a double holster with a fancy set of custom-made Colts. He checked and loaded each of the weapons, then buckled on the guns and called to Ace Dawson to accompany him. The others he dismissed with the wave of his hand.

Dawson promised to join him at the back of the saloon in a moment; a promise he had no intention of keeping until he had taken certain precautions. First Dawson raced down the street to Flynn's Saloon. This establishment was the hangout of a gang that Morgan frequently employed for special jobs. Headed by one Big Jim, they were as ferocious a bunch of cutthroats as ever banded together; their allegiance loosely owed to Big Jim. He, in turn, was loyal to Morgan for the jobs that the chief threw his way.

Dawson figured that Big Jim would come quickly to the aid of Jack in this emergency. When he pushed through the swinging doors he was amazed to see that the table where Big Jim and his gang usually sat was empty. He went to the proprietor who stood polishing glasses behind the bar.

'Where's Big Jim and his bunch, Flynn?' asked Ace.

'Rode out half an hour ago when they heard about Pop. Left their drinks just like yuh see 'em there—half-finished.'

'Were they scared?'

'No. I wouldn't say they was scared. Nothin' could scare that bunch. Yuh see, they'd been talkin' about the luck Morgan's been havin'. They sort of made their minds up that Morgan's luck was all run out.'

Dawson stared blankly at the table, with its round of half-finished drinks and a still-smoldering cigar.

'The town is talkin' Ace, and yuh'll find a lot o' folks that has taken a fancy to them two!'

'*Two*? What do you mean—"them two"?' He glared at the bartender. 'Do you mean Leach and Barnes?'

'Them's the two.'

'*They* didn't get Winters!' declared Ace.

'How do yuh know?' asked Flynn, holding a polished glass up to the light and then wiping away an imaginary speck.

''Cause they was takin' care of Red Calhoun at the time.'

'But I heered Abe Leach did that hisself,' reminded Flynn.

Dawson glared at the proprietor and, turning on his heel, strode from the barroom. Once outside, he paused and stood leaning against one of the posts that held up the long veranda.

Perhaps, he thought, some deep reflection would be appropriate at this time.

He looked down the street toward the far end. That street was a hangout of fighting men. There were no less than twelve saloons and gambling houses strung along the way, and from early morning until late at night the number of tough mustangs ordinarily hitched there, while their gun-hung riders drank and gambled inside, would seldom go below fifty. But now the street, unbelievably, contained not a single mount that could be called the horse of a fighting man!

Ace decided not to join Morgan immediately, but first to investigate things at the nearest livery stable. He walked to the huge barn, noting the absence of horses in the corral. The proprietor was carrying gear from a large pile near the door to the inside. The pile contained blanket rolls, saddles, rifles and cooking pots—even pistols and rifles.

'How's business, Ike?' asked Dawson eyeing the pile. He thought he had recognized a rifle.

'Business is brisk.'

'A lot of customers comin' in?'

'Hell, no! They's a-goin' *out*! Sold every horse in the corral; even had to go out in the pasture to get more.' He paused to pick up an armload of rifles which he carted inside, with Dawson following. 'Never see a bunch o' boys so eager to get their hands on a hoss. Them that

191

didn't have the cash was a-giving away rifles, guns and stuff at cut-rate prices.'

'Let me get this straight, Ikc,' said Dawson, grabbing the other by the arm and bringing him to a halt. 'You mean that you sold every nag you got in this stable—even that old pot-bellied, gray-whiskered plough hoss?'

'Shore did, Ace,' acknowledged the other, going back for an armload of pistols. 'I'm in the gun business now, it looks like.'

'What caused it, Ike?'

'Wal, that's got me beat to hell. I can only tell ya that when those who had hosses began to stampede outa here, them that didn't have mounts began to acquire them.'

'Get my horse ready,' said Ace Dawson, 'I'm gonna ride out an' see what this is all about.'

Ace Dawson picked up his blanket roll and all the cash he had on hand. He had decided that he might have a happier winter in some quiet town up north; perhaps Montana would be far enough away.

CHAPTER SEVENTEEN

Jack Morgan was enjoying himself in the small courtyard behind Rielly's Saloon as he scrambled about, reading sign of the battle. He was happy when he discovered the piece of the grip of a Colt revolver. It was from a fancy weapon such as Luke Barnes had carried. And he found a small handful of dog hairs clinging to a burr.

As he paced about the area, his foot struck a hollow note on one of the flagstones. In an instant he was on hands and knees, raising the stone and peering down into the passage. This discovery rallied his hopes and he smiled triumphantly. From his pocket he took a small tube on which he slid back a shutter and lighted the wick with a match. With the miniature lantern he climbed into the tunnel.

Morgan explored the passages; he found the fireplace entrance to Rielly's room at once and briefly looked within. In the room under the bar he carefully examined everything, including the trap door into the barroom. Morgan gently tested the door and found it to be free. Smiling, he remembered how he had shifted the heavy hogshead over this very door.

Next, he carefully examined every detail of the room and its contents, noting the spots where the former occupants rubbed against dusty places, the crumbs left from food recently served, the tobacco leavings, and the prints on the dusty floor. From his observations he concluded that Abe Leach and Luke had performed their escape by riding in the front door, dismounting and whipping the horses out the back, and then dropping out of sight through the trap door behind the bar.

Of course, he realized now that only Rielly could have brought the food to them from the part of the passage that led to her room. Also, it became apparent that Abe Leach had known of the tunnel, and had met Rielly there before.

Morgan laughed softly as he remembered the subtle way in which Rielly had wheedled him into inviting her to join in the chase, then had cleverly arranged to bring the horses to the back door. The pieces of rope showed that Pop Winters had recently found the passage and that his captor had been Luke Barnes, accompanied on the patio by a large dog.

Morgan threw his head back and roared with laughter as he pictured the expression on Jane Rielly's face when he confronted her with his discoveries. He decided that he would dally with her no longer, and laughed again loud and long, knowing that the sound probably was carrying up through the floor and, weirdly distorted by echoes, frightening the wits out of Rielly's customers.

Satisfied, he hurried out of the passage, carefully replaced the flagstone, and entered the saloon by the back door.

Inside, the patrons were still uneasily looking from one to the other and wondering about the source of the mysterious, unearthly-sounding laughter.

The bartender was frozen in the position of

wiping the bar, the poker game was at a standstill—in fact, Morgan's brisk entrance was the first movement in a minute and a half. Rielly had been arranging some flowers on the piano, the piano player had paused to listen for more.

With the appearance of the formidable Morgan, conversation came back in a flood; the bartender proceeded to wipe, the piano player took up his tune and the poker players began to play. Merely by being there, Morgan brought back their courage; with him in the room they all felt immeasurably safer.

Morgan strode to the bar, where the bartender, anticipating his coming, set up a small brandy glass and poured it to the brim from his own special bottle. Rielly came to his side.

'Good evening, John,' she said, searching his face for a clue.

'Good evening, my dear. Let's go down here to the end of the bar, shall we?' he said, escorting her there.

He looked deeply into her eyes. 'We can watch the trap door so clearly from here!'

Rielly reeled as he stared her down.

'My dear, it's quite a game you've been playing behind my back, but you see I'm clever, too. We'll be getting married tonight, up in your room. I'll send for the judge, and if you like, we can go off on our honeymoon through the fireplace.'

Rielly gasped and grabbed at the bar.

'We should make quite a combination; with your ability to scheme, and my own talents, we'll do all right. I've been liquidating my assets for some weeks now, and this is a good time to leave Denver—after I have taken care of your playmates.'

Rielly broke away and ran for her room. Morgan laughed after her and raising his glass, drank deeply. As he drank, his eyes were riveted on the face above the swinging doors. Slowly he lowered the glass.

'Come in, Mr. Barnes; come in.'

'You're under arrest, Morgan,' said Luke, elbowing his way through the door and into the room.

Fifteen paces separated them. The people in the room took the cover that was closest; the piano player dove behind his instrument, the bartender flattened himself in his refuge; the poker players turned their table over and peeked gingerly from their fortress. Rielly had disappeared.

'Ah,' smiled Morgan. 'Under arrest? What is the charge?'

'Murder, robbery, rustlin', forgery, hoss-thieving', smugglin', kidnapin', gun-runnin', claim-jumpin', grave-robbin', an' assault on federal officers,' came the string of charges from

Marshal Abe Leach, standing behind Morgan in the rear doorway.

'Interesting!'

'Watch his hands, Luke,' called the marshal, taking a step toward Morgan.

Morgan flicked his shoulder and threw a shot backward, crumpling Abe Leach in his tracks. He had used the big mirror behind the bar to aim. As Luke made his draw, his eyes went to Abe Leach for perhaps the fifth part of a second; he saw the blood appear above the star on the marshal's chest. Morgan had neatly clipped off one of the five points of the star.

In the fraction of time that Luke had looked away, Morgan had shifted his position by a good ten feet. Morgan fired, but the change of position worked against him. The bullet that he aimed for the space between Luke's eyes missed its mark by a good three inches.

Luke was blinded for a minute as Morgan's bullet creased the side of his head. His legs went limp and his knees sagged, his gun, never clear of the holster, dropped back into the leather. As he blinked and the image of the room came clear once more, Morgan was upon him with fists slashing at his face.

Morgan knocked him staggering as Luke tried vainly to bob out of the way. He held on as Handsome Jack pounded his ribs with sledge-hammer blows; after the first smashing blasts to his head, the punishing body attack was welcome to Luke. His head cleared and he could see the weaving, grim-visaged Morgan, methodically choosing the spots for his blows to land.

One look into Morgan's eyes and Luke could see the intent of the man was to beat him to death. He took good aim at Morgan's jaw and putting all his strength into it, zipped his right, flush onto the point of Morgan's chin.

To say that Luke was disappointed with the effects of the punch would be putting it mildly. His hand ached and Morgan grinned back, but Luke got a grip on the shirt of the other. He pulled his adversary off balance and smashed him on the ear. The shirt sleeve he ripped clean off and the blow hurt Morgan; for a brief moment he saw Morgan start to reach for the red ear, then the master renegade tore into the fray.

Morgan hurled a chair with all his might. Luke managed to parry it and get in a good kick at the killer's leg; the kick he followed up with a right-cross. His knuckles caught the loose skin of Morgan's lips and, tearing the lower flap, brought forth a spurt of blood.

Panting heavily, Luke paused. His shirt was hanging in tatters, his face a bloody pulp.

Arms hanging, Morgan labored for great breaths of air. Suddenly he drew a long knife and crept forward, circling to the right.

Luke moved away, circling to the left. He drew his knife just in time to parry a slashing attack by the outlaw, but he felt the keen point bite into the tight skin across his chest, and saw the red on Morgan's blade. Luke desperately flung his knife as he circled, and his hopes fell as it went spinning past Morgan's head and out over the swinging doors. Then Luke stumbled over an overturned chair and went sprawling on his back. He looked up just as Morgan aimed the knife at his heart.

Morgan smiled and wiped off the blade, returning it to its sheath. Slowly, it seemed to Luke, he drew a revolver and took point-blank aim. Luke stunned at this maneuver, clutched for his pistol. But he knew he would never be fast enough. He watched the cylinder of Morgan's gun turn as the renegade chief drew back the hammer and prepared for deliberate, cold-blooded murder.

Luke's gun cleared his holster a shade too late as the other gun exploded.

★   ★   ★

Of course, Luke knew, it was Rielly who fired the shot that killed Jack Morgan. First of all, thanks to her father's training, she was an excellent shot with both rifle and pistol; and secondly, she was the only other person who knew of the existence of the peephole in the passage from which she had fired the shot. Luke had managed to fire his gun, and every man present swore that it was his shot that had torn the heart from Jack Morgan. No one had noticed the separate reports, so close did the shots follow one another!

Abe Leach recovered quickly, for the badge that had been his life deflected the bullet, which had plowed along his ribs and popped harmlessly out his side.

There was evidence in great quantity among Morgan's belongings and this, along with certain records that the renegade chief had kept, helped to prove to the most trusting the wickedness of the man.

Luke and Rielly never did explain about the twin shots—by mutual consent. Abe Leach recovered soon enough to overtake Ace Dawson a thousand miles later; Ace Dawson, the last of the Inner Circle, surrendered to the lawman quite peaceably by mutual consent. Luke and Rielly have a big ranch outside Denver and two fine sons that are watched over by a great white dog. The boys are named Abe and John—by mutual consent.